THE OBITUARY WRITER

THE OBITUARY WRITER

PORTER SHREVE

A MARINER ORIGINAL
HOUGHTON MIFFLIN COMPANY
Boston · New York
2000

For information about permission to reproduce
selections from this book, write to Permissions,
Houghton Mifflin Company, 215 Park Avenue South,
New York, New York 10003.

Visit our Web site: www.hmco.com/trade.

Library of Congress Cataloging-in-Publication Data
Shreve, Porter.
The obituary writer / Porter Shreve.
p.   cm.
"A Mariner Original."
ISBN 0-395-98132-8
I. Title.
PS3569.H7395 O25 2000
813'.54 — dc21   99-046759

Printed in the United States of America

Book design by Robert Overholtzer

QUM 10 9 8 7 6 5 4 3 2 1

for my mother

I WOULD LIKE TO THANK

my editor, Wendy Holt; my agent, Joe Regal; the Meijer
Foundation, the Colby Fellowship, the Avery Hopwood and
Jule Hopwood Fund; Louie Estrada, Lisa Estrada,
Jeff Avery, Jessica Avery, Khoi Nguyen, Jeff Richards,
and my MFA teachers and workshop at
the University of Michigan.

———————

I am especially grateful to my family — Dad, Carol,
Sooz, Tim, Liz, Rusty, Caleb, Kate — and to Bich.

1

MY FATHER, who died when I was five, had a reputation as a great newspaperman. I never doubted that I could be one too. "It's a matter of destiny," my mother would say to me with her usual drama. I believed her, and that's where my trouble began.

I was eight when I took my first paper route — three hundred houses with the *Columbia Pioneer* at ninety-five dollars a week. That first winter, my mother delivered the papers with me. She woke me at five in the morning dressed in a scarf, sweatshirt and jogging pants, white moon boots, and her old camel-hair coat, and we went out into darkness to the corner of Stadium and La Grange to pick up the bundles. On certain days the distributors would leave inserts — the home section on Tuesdays, real estate on Fridays, comics, coupons, classifieds, and *Parade* for the Sunday paper — and my mother and I would sit on the cold floor of the garage putting inserts and headsheets together, folding the papers in thirds, slipping them into plastic sleeves.

When we had folded and bagged all three hundred papers, my mother popped the hatchback of what was then her brand-new 1975 AMC Gremlin, brown with a white racing stripe. We stacked the papers in the back of the car, then sat in the front, waiting in silence as the Gremlin warmed up. This was the best time of the day.

The silence, the murkiness of first light, the warm air from the heater closing around us.

By the time I was twelve, I was collecting newspapers. I'd save one a day from my morning route, and my mother, Lorraine, who was a secretary at the University of Missouri Journalism School, would bring home thumbed-through discards from the school library. I kept a handwritten log of what stories I deemed important, by date and subject, from the *New York Times, Chicago Tribune,* and *Dallas Morning News.* The papers piled up in labeled stacks in the garage, until eventually I had so many that my mother had to park her car in the driveway. This must have been an inconvenience, since we had limited space, but she wasn't about to let an AMC Gremlin, which smelled of engine oil when you turned on the heat, roll over my dreams.

I grew up with a heightened sense of my own importance, which my mother encouraged. She figured an only child with a single parent ought to be treated as exceptional. "Great men like your father come along only rarely," she liked to say, beginning an exhortation I'd hear many times throughout my youth, often following the arrival of more bad news from school.

I'd come home from basketball, a skinny sixteen, and she'd be standing by the microwave lining Triscuits onto a plate, slicing cheese to melt on top. I'd go to the refrigerator for a soda and see my final grades taped to the door.

"Some who are born great fall through the cracks," she'd say, waving the knife in a backhand motion, narrowing her wide-set eyes on me. "Maybe they end up homeless. Maybe dead. Maybe they go crazy. Who knows? If you're born great, the rule is: you soar to the sun or you sink to the silt."

Pale and narrow, the bones in her downturned face just beneath her skin, my mother would often strike me as youth standing at the boundary of old age. I'd watch her turn in the crinkly black dress that sharpened her features and darkened her eyes and wonder if men in town found her pretty. She'd walk to the stove, rigid and deliberate, and roll a cigarette in the flame.

"Einstein flunked math when he was your age, but he got his act together and they gave him the Nobel Prize." She'd take a couple of nervous puffs, lighting her cigarette unevenly. "These grades are unacceptable, Gordie, but let me say this: you have the substance of greatness."

Even on my mother's salary, we could have afforded a better place, something I never tired of bringing up. We had lived in the same Sears, Roebuck house at 102 La Grange since I was five, always with boarding students stomping above us. Our half of the house had low ceilings and little light, and though it was kept clean, nothing had changed in years. The living room was small, with a lumpy yellow sofa, shag carpet, a near-empty curio cabinet, and a fall-apart rocking chair that I was forever salvaging with Super Glue. We ate in the kitchen at a Formica dinette under cheerful aphorisms that my mother would copy out of magazines and hang on the walls.

My room had always looked the same, even later when I came home to visit, as it did when I was a boy: the comforter on the bed printed with old headlines: TITANIC SINKS, SACCO AND VANZETTI GUILTY, LINDBERGH BABY KIDNAPPED; the basketball trophy for best playmaker in summer camp atop my writing desk; the same photographs on the walls: my father, a cigarette hanging from his lip, his eyes squinting from the smoke, in the newsroom; my mother on their wedding day in Norfolk, Virginia, leaning stiffly against a newel post in elbow-length gloves; Harry Truman, the pride of Missouri, with a big gray smile famously lofting the *Chicago Tribune;* and a picture of me and my father taken on Easter Sunday, 1972, eight weeks before he died.

I cherished this picture because I had an actual memory of the scene. The cloudless sky, the pale grass on an uncommonly warm spring day. My father, Charlie Hatch, thirty-six years old, sitting on the back stairs of my uncle's house in Wichita in a blue and white seersucker suit with a Panama hat brim-down over his head. I remember my mother chasing me with a camera while I ran around the yard making airplane noises, my arms outstretched. Out of the blue my uncle had snatched me up and whispered conspiratorially in my ear, "I'm going to zoom you at your daddy and you're going to take his hat."

The photograph, a grainy black and white, captures the scene a minute later. My father, hatless, his back to the camera, bends above me, looking over his shoulder. I'm sitting upright on the lawn in a white shirt. The Panama hat rests hugely over my head.

My mother and I were for the most part alone. She did sometimes have company over, small potlucks with friends from the office, but usually we had the evenings to ourselves. I'd organize my newspapers in the garage or write long editorials at my desk for no one's eyes but mine, while my mother played her light operas too loud on the RCA Victor my father had given her. She had a singular passion for Gilbert and Sullivan and knew every word to *The Gondoliers, Princess Ida,* and *The Pirates of Penzance.* She'd twirl around the room or hum along as she read *Cosmopolitan* in the fall-apart rocking chair.

My mother kept no photographs of my father in the living room. What mementos she did have were locked away in her bedroom, down the dark hallway from mine. The few times I went in there as a child, I felt an immediate urge to turn back. Her small room had no carpeting, and the creak in the wood, the shock of the cold floor on my bare feet, gave me a feeling of emptiness.

The double bed was always made, with a brown chenille spread pulled taut over the single pillow and tucked in all around like a private's bunk. Hanging above it, in a thick wooden frame, was a needlepoint sampler of flowers and vines surrounding the words GROW WHERE YOU ARE PLANTED.

Against one wall was a heavy walnut dresser; atop it, neatly arranged in saucers, lay pennies and nickels and Viceroy cigarettes. In the far corner sat an old rolltop desk, always locked, where I assumed my father's things were saved: his wallet, his press pass, his obituary from the major papers, all the photographs, many with important people, letters and keepsakes from his life with my mother, clips from his short but dazzling career.

My father's first job out of the Navy was on the city desk at the *Wichita Kansan*. Back in the early sixties a midrange paper sent out maybe a dozen reporters, and the cub, my father at the time, usually got the police beat. He checked in with the hospitals, kept contact with the precincts, and reported to accidents, robberies, and the occasional homicide, where he'd call his stories back to the office for rewrite. He liked the work but, according to my mother, he was restless. He wanted to make an impact on the world, and toward the end of 1963, eight months into the job, his opportunity arrived.

In those days, the Associated Press put out a calendar of upcoming national events every other Thursday, and late one November afternoon my father picked off the wires the news that President Kennedy would be in Dallas the next day. He was off Friday and Saturday, so he called my mother and cut out of work early and bought a ticket on the five-fifteen Silversides Thruliner, the overnight bus to Dallas.

The next morning at Love Field, awaiting Kennedy's arrival, my father weaved through the crowd to a cordoned-off press area right up front just as the President and the First Lady were appearing at the door of Air Force One. President Kennedy descended the metal staircase, walked up to the press area and the cheerful throng that had gathered to greet him. Of all the hands extended, he chose my father's.

For a moment that must have replayed in his mind every day

for the rest of his life, my father held the President's hand and looked straight into his blue eyes, squinting in the bright noon sun.

As the presidential limousine pulled away, with its plastic bubbletop removed and bulletproof windows rolled down on account of the glorious weather, my father, not giving it a second thought, squeezed in with the press pool, which followed six cars behind the President in a telephone company van.

The van was turning a corner when three shots cracked the sky over downtown Dallas, and my father witnessed it all: the President's limousine, a hundred yards ahead, slowing down and weaving in the road; the flurry of activity in the Secret Service follow-up car; the spot of pink that he'd later recognize as the First Lady crawling across the long black trunk.

Suddenly the President's car sped off and the van driver followed it, passing the Vice President's car, racing out onto the highway to Parkland Hospital.

My father saw President Kennedy's body wheeled toward the emergency room. He saw the horror-stricken expression on the face of the man pushing the gurney. He saw two priests hurry down the hospital corridor with purple stoles wrapped tightly in their hands and a policeman rush by with a heavy carton of blood for transfusions. He was there, at the hospital, at 1:33 P.M., when a press aide announced that the President of the United States was dead.

"That's the fate of the exceptional journalists," my mother would say, recounting the story. "They're lodestones of history."

In the days following the Kennedy assassination, my father's byline reached not only the *Kansan* but the *Kansas City Star* and newspapers all over the Midwest. He stayed on the story for two years, covering the Warren Commission investigation and the Jack Ruby trial, leaving the *Kansan* for the *Chicago Tribune*, where he headed a special Dallas bureau until the dust began to settle. By the time he moved to Chicago in 1965, the year before I was born, he was already a star.

I stayed home, in Columbia, for college, and my mother made a great show of loading up the Gremlin and driving me the quarter mile to my dormitory room on the University of Missouri campus. At the journalism school, I thrived, tackling regular assignments for the *Columbia Missourian,* the school's daily paper. I won an annual reporting award for my series about the effect of deinstitutionalization on the local homeless. For this, my mother gave me my father's briefcase, a weathered oxblood London Courier, still edged with newspaper ink.

In the summer of my junior year, I landed an internship with the *St. Louis Independent,* where I returned after graduation to work as an editorial assistant. A slot opened up on the obituary desk when another young reporter left for the night police beat. And on the fourteenth of August, 1988, exactly three months before my twenty-second birthday, the *Independent* promoted me to full-time obituary writer.

From my corner of the newsroom I believed that I could be a lodestone too. I merely had to hunker down, work hard, and await the inevitable.

2

THE *St. Louis Independent* was a morning paper with a circulation of 305,000, the twenty-ninth-largest daily in America. Many around the journalism school and in the national press considered it the last of a dying breed, a true old-fashioned newspaper, neither sentimental nor cynical, but reflecting the famous "show me" skepticism of the state of Missouri. The *Independent* had grown out of the ashes of the *Missouri Gazette,* the first North American newspaper published west of the Mississippi River. The pioneering spirit of the *Gazette's* founder, Joseph Charless, who in 1808 had pulled the first edition of his paper from an old Ramage press and delivered it himself, lived on at the *Independent.* Our logo, overarched by the Missouri state motto — "The Welfare of the People Shall Be the Supreme Law" — was a lithograph of Charless working his hand-operated press.

I admired the paper's history, was proud to work in a place that seemed to back the underdog. Growing up, I had followed the *Independent's* many battles with Monsanto, the multibillion-dollar chemical company across the river in East St. Louis, which had introduced PCBs, dioxin, and Agent Orange to the world, to go along with its more "beneficial" products, like saccharine, Nutrasweet, and dairy hormones. Unswayed by Monsanto's advertising dollars and its power in the region, the *Independent* ran series after series in the early eighties exposing the deadly contamination that Monsanto's manufacturing had brought upon East St. Louis. Thanks in part to the *Independent,* the national press began for the first time to think of the environment as front-page news.

The *Independent*'s offices took up seven floors of an industrial-era steel and concrete building that loomed directly above the International Bowling Museum and Hall of Fame, home to Earl Anthony, Dick Weber, Floretta McCutcheon, and other legends of the lanes, in downtown St. Louis. Most days I arrived before anyone else in the newsroom. The elevator up to the sixth floor would be full of the eight-to-four crowd, on their way to Classified, Accounting, Circulation, or Personnel. I would stand in a back corner, listening to bits of other departments' gossip — who was dating whom, who got canned, who was too ambitious for his own good — as the creaky elevator stopped at each floor. One month a new elevator was installed, with an intercom that spoke in a woman's voice. "Please stand back," she said gently. "Going up." Such instances of modernity were rare in our offices.

It was the sixth floor, though, that harbored all of the tension and adrenaline of news reporting that I craved, and where, as absurd as it seemed, I thought I could detect my father's presence. He would descend as a kind of heat, a shiver across my scalp and down my spine. Sometimes I'd swear I could sense him looking out through my eyes, a young reporter waiting for the flare in the sky that points to the great discovery. I'd stop at the rackety wire machines under the mural of Remington's *Pony Express* to scroll through the overnight news, then pick up a late edition from the stacks before taking the long, slow route to my desk.

Along the east wall the managing and assistant managing editors had offices with sweeping views of downtown. Jim St. John headed up the metro section, and had the largest office. A small man with a wiry mustache who wore brown suits and galaxy ties, St. John had a booming voice and a morbid sense of humor. Without fail, at five o'clock each day when I stepped into his office with a list of the next day's obits, he would swivel in his chair and reach out his hand, saying, "Give us this day our daily dead."

The editors and writers for the metro section covered the middle of the newsroom. Metro had the largest staff, the biggest budget, its own investigative unit, and a dozen special beats; it was the training ground for the national post in Washington and the foreign desk in London — and where I very much hoped to be.

My desk, nestled between a thick column and a huge clattering overhead fan, was at the end of the last row of metro clusters. The fan marked the terminus of a vast network of tubing which looked like a Bauhaus air-conditioning duct but served the purpose of transferring lead particles to a work site on the floor below. The lead removal program had been ongoing since my arrival fourteen months earlier, slated then to last another six months. One day a yellow sign was posted above my desk: LEAD REMOVAL NEARING COMPLETION, BUT DON'T HOLD YOUR BREATH.

Two of us worked on obits: myself and Dick Ritger, a twenty-year veteran of the *Independent* who had once been editorial page editor and now wore a mouth guard so he wouldn't chew himself from the inside out. As a result we rarely talked. When I had arrived, he had been writing obits for a year and a half and his jaw had been wired shut. The cause of Ritger's downfall was anybody's guess. He had few friends in the newsroom, and everyone had a different opinion about what had happened. Post-traumatic stress, cocaine, a double life about to be exposed. Something from his past, quite literally, gnawed at him. Before the newsroom ban on cigarettes four years ago, Ritger had been a chain smoker, and when he could no longer light up in the conference room, he quit, cold turkey, and started filling his mouth with gumballs.

Before the breakdown, Ritger was by all reports a classic, why-because-I-said-so newspaperman. He had a gravelly voice and a bad temper. His favorite word was "asshole." His face went from crimson to purple depending on the time of day, and he was bald but for a band of close-cropped gray hairs. His physical deterioration, however, belied his sense of style. Tall and trim, he wore fine tailored suits, perforated black suspenders, and pointy Italian shoes.

When the gumballs no longer worked, when, as one of his colleagues at Editorial explained it, "he looked as if his head would explode," Ritger checked himself into the hospital. Diagnosed with an extreme condition of tooth grinding, which if unchecked would eventually wear away the dentin and expose the nerves, he took three months to recuperate. An announcement was left on the office bulletin board explaining the situation, giving the address of a rehabilitation center where flowers and good wishes could be sent.

When Ritger returned to work in a neck brace and with his jaw wired shut, the editorial page had a new editor. Within a week another young obituary writer had been promoted, and Ritger was placed in the vacant slot. That young obituary writer was now one of two metro reporters covering the demonstrations in Eastern Europe. It had taken him just a year and a half to make it — enough to give a young reporter hope.

I had been working long hours, coming in on weekends and staying late, helping the ad people compile death notices, getting my name out to funeral directors, scouring the wires for recent deaths. I wrote thirty of the forty obituaries that ran each week, leaving a handful for Ritger, who seemed interested only in writing up decorated veterans and old-school journalists.

Secretly, I had started the *Independent*'s first archive of prewritten obituaries, which I saved in my personal computer file, accessible to no one else, under the trade name "advancers." Every morning until eleven, when Ritger steamed in, and evenings from seven until ten, I worked exclusively on obituaries of the not yet departed.

My first advancers were the four living American Presidents. I'd search *Who's Who, Lexis-Nexis, Current Biography,* and library clip files, taking four workdays and parts of the weekend to write each thirty-inch piece. Aging world leaders came next: the Pope, Deng, François Mitterrand; then entertainers: Bette Davis, Leonard Bernstein; then Nobelists, writers, athletes, and so forth. I wanted to stockpile as many advancers as possible, but at the same time I prided myself on crafting elegant mini-biographies that would make readers wish they had known the person.

When advancers crept their way back into the headlines, I'd have to make updates. A particular nuisance was Jimmy Carter, with his international peacemaking, forcing me finally, after a dozen revisions, to give up on the idea of keeping his file current. By the time he died, I figured, I'd be miles from the obituary desk.

On the morning of Alicia Whiting's phone call, in my customary first ritual of the day, I counted seventy-nine prewritten obits queuing in my archive. As of yet, however, I'd had no occasion to use one.

She called at a quarter to five on Saturday, October 5, fifteen minutes before a tight deadline for the Sunday paper. Little distinguished this day from any other. Emerson Electric's chief financial officer had died overnight and the business desk had requested a third of our allotted space. I was on hold with a funeral director, checking facts and at the same time reducing the life of a Wentzville dentist to one column, eleven inches.

"This is Arthur Whiting's wife," the woman said in a regional accent that I couldn't place. "You've probably been expecting my call."

I wrote the name on the back of a press release, put her on hold, and paused for a moment with the phone on my shoulder. I'd never heard of Arthur Whiting. I checked the space budget list to see if he was scheduled for the next day, flipped through some recent wire printouts, opened the paper to the obit page.

"What was your husband's name again?"

"Arthur Russell Whiting."

I asked if she knew this was the obituary desk.

"Of course. I assume your people were trying to reach me today. Well, I was out. I wanted to be gone when the press arrived."

She sounded too young, too self-controlled to be a widow.

"My husband, Arthur Whiting," she repeated his name in her calm, insistent voice, "was a man of consequence."

I told her I was sorry and to please hold again, then stood up to scan the newsroom for Ritger. I walked over to Editorial, where he sometimes went to make old colleagues nervous, but he wasn't there. I checked the east wall and stopped by the main stairwell and called his name from the banister. Not wanting to bother anyone furiously typing away on deadline, I went back to my desk and sat down heavily, wondering how someone "of consequence" could have escaped my memory.

I called the librarian in Research, asked him to pull up anything he could find on an Arthur Whiting, closed the computer file on the Wentzville dentist, and told the funeral home that I'd call them back.

"Not to worry," Mrs. Whiting said as I returned to the phone, apologizing for making her wait. "I understand how it is with busy people. Arthur was a busy man."

Her accent was distinctive but still unfamiliar. It had neither the languor of Kansas City and St. Louis nor the twang of the towns in between. I would have said it was Southern, but there was a touch of the stage actress as well that made it sound more refined — the way she said "not to worry," the breathiness of "Arthur." In journalism school, broadcast people were taught to speak a certain way, and I always found it sad hearing kids my age from Texas and Arkansas bury their regional accents. Alicia Whiting's voice had that same distilled quality.

"We'll have a large number for the funeral. Hundreds, I suppose," she said. "There's so much to get ready before Tuesday."

Whiting, I was thinking to myself. I knew a construction company with blue signs and a cityscape logo. I'd seen one hanging off a crane just this morning.

"I have to put the service together all by myself," she went on. "I'll order white roses. Definitely, white roses."

I opened the Yellow Pages to Concrete — Construction — Contractors. WILEY, one of the bigger ads read. BUILDING FOR THE FUTURE SINCE 1948.

"Arthur had excellent taste," she was saying. "We aren't rich, but what we have is of good quality."

I slid the phone book back into my desk.

"Our Irish wolfhound placed at Westminster last year. That's at Madison Square Garden in New York City. I don't know why people make such a big deal. I really don't care for New York City."

I looked at the clock — a minute to five — and typed her name in the new file. Besides reducing the Wentzville dentist's obit, I had to finish fact-checking with one funeral home and call another to confirm a death, a formality I rarely left to the last minute. I had yet to update the space budget list or alert Layout that we'd need a more recent picture of the Emerson Electric CFO. It wasn't wise for someone in my position to be late on a Saturday for the early-run Sunday paper. But I was strangely unfocused listening to this woman, running "Whiting" over the contours of my memory.

"What's your name?" she asked.

I paused a moment before telling her, mindful of the journalistic protocol of keeping things impersonal.

"I always like to know who I'm talking to," she explained. "I'm Alicia Whiting."

The research librarian called on the other line. I put Mrs. Whiting back on hold. "We've got two clips," he said. "The first one's about a bank robbery. Arthur Whiting was assistant manager at a Portage Savings in Creve Coeur. He tripped the alarm and was hero for the day. Front page of Metro's got a picture of him. The caption reads, 'He had never been so scared . . . blah, blah, blah.'

"There's a quote here about how he kept reaching for the button and missing it, and his boss says some nice things about him. The second clip's about a dog show."

"What are the dates?" I asked.

"The bank one's from 1984, the dog show's last February. I'll bring them over."

I got back on the phone with Mrs. Whiting. I knew I sounded rushed. "I'm sorry. Our deadline is five o'clock, and I have several things left to wrap up."

She said she didn't mind holding. And for a split second her disarming calm — why she had gone on sharing such odd details of her life — made me believe I was dealing with a woman paralyzed by grief.

At quarter past I tapped on the glass door of St. John's office expecting a reprimand for being late, but the back of his high-backed chair didn't move. His secretary said he'd been gone much of the day and probably wouldn't make the six-thirty meeting. I left her the list of the next day's obituaries and asked if she had seen Ritger. "He went home sick," she said. "Just after lunch."

Waiting on my desk were the picture and the two clips on Arthur Whiting, all the paper had from the past ten years, and one was about a dog show. This "man of consequence" had turned out to be an ordinary guy. Strange how quickly I had doubted myself. Others had gotten through to the desk before when I was on deadline — grieving widows, irascible family members, parents of accident victims — but it rarely took more than a few minutes for me to say what I had to say: "Our deadline is final. We can't do it until tomorrow," even if tomorrow meant the time and location of the service wouldn't appear until the day of the funeral, even if tomorrow was too late. So why hadn't I done the same with Alicia Whiting?

The hold button was still flashing. It had been twenty minutes.

"Are you still there?" I asked.

"Yes." Her voice didn't reveal a hint of irritation.

"Mrs. Whiting," I began.

"Alicia," she said.

"I'm afraid the deadline for tomorrow's paper has passed." I tried to sound resolute. "You'll have to call back in the morning."

"St. Louis is a nice city," she said sadly. "I like it here, but I should probably leave."

"I know," I said in an effort to hurry her along, now convinced that my instincts had been right. This was a woman in shock. There was the clink of ice and a sound like breathing into a glass, and I wondered if she might be drinking.

"I used to drive around and feel like this was my very own city. The streets were my streets and the river was mine and the barges and riverboats. And the buildings, too. Especially the buildings. I'd walk up and down the stairs of the old post office and run my hand over the banisters or sit in the main reading room of the public library looking up at the high ceilings, like they were ceilings in my own house. But I don't feel that way anymore."

"I'm sorry," I said.

"I just want to stay home now, and my house is small. Fall is the best time of year, when the leaves start to change. Arthur liked to take me on walks in the botanical gardens."

This woman had waited for twenty minutes. Twenty minutes I'd had her on hold and she didn't even mention it. This must be despair, I thought, going to such lengths to keep a stranger on the phone.

The fan clattered away on its evening cycle. Apart from the racket, it cast a noxious odor, especially at this time of day when the lead particles, having accumulated from all corners of the newsroom, made a final turn from my desk on their way to the lower floor.

"What's that noise?" she asked.

As if on cue, the fan abruptly stopped.

"You should call us in the morning," I said, making use of the pause. "If you'd like to gather the information and fax it, with place of residence, age, occupation, cause of death —"

"Let me give it to you now," she interrupted.

And I realized that I wouldn't stand firm, that I was losing this fight, had lost it in fact an hour ago when I was convinced somehow of her husband's importance, then drawn in by the loneliness in her voice. I took down the essentials and promised I'd do my best to get it into the next morning's paper. With Ritger not looming over me, it wouldn't be much trouble finding space for a small obit. And that's exactly what I did — tapped out five inches, no subhead, fourth column, below the fold:

Arthur R. Whiting, 43, a loan officer with Portage Savings Bank, died Friday of a heart attack at his home in St. Charles.

Mr. Whiting was born in Davenport, Iowa. He was graduated from the University of Iowa in Iowa City with a degree in business administration. He also served in the U.S. Army.

Mr. Whiting was employed by Portage Savings Bank for 15 years. He worked as a bank teller, assistant manager, and manager before becoming chief loan officer at the St. Charles South branch.

He was treasurer of the Whispering Pines Country Club and former treasurer of the Clayton Lodge of Elks. A dog enthusiast, Mr. Whiting owned Irish wolfhounds that won several local, state, and national awards.

He leaves his wife, Alicia; a brother, Joseph R., of Winfield; and a sister, Margaret M., of St. Charles.

I hit Save and made a few more cuts to the dentist's obit to make room. I hadn't eaten since breakfast and could feel the dizziness that sets in with extreme hunger. I brought up a plate of rice and some kind of goulash from the cafeteria, forwarded my calls to the switchboard operator, and devoured my dinner, staring at the green blur of letters on my computer screen. I was in no mood to stay late, having wrapped up an advancer on Joe DiMaggio late the night before. So I packed up my briefcase, and getting up to leave, noticed Arthur Whiting's picture and the two clips still sitting on my desk.

In the picture, Alicia's husband was standing in front of the

Portage Savings Bank shaking a policeman's hand. Tall and stoop-shouldered, he had thinning hair, rather long in the back, and a discernibly large Adam's apple. He looked older than forty-three, rawboned and hollow-cheeked.

The bank robbery had occurred just as the librarian described it. Arthur had gone for the emergency button, couldn't find it until the last possible moment. A pair of squad cars happened to be a block away, and the dispatcher had the police there in minutes. The robber was sixty-eight years old and had no accomplices. "It's not often a criminal is active at that age, much less still alive," an officer was quoted as saying.

The dog-show clip was short, a three-inch brief in Hannah Greene's "At Home and Around Town" column:

> NEW YORK — An Irish wolfhound from St. Charles has won a top prize at the famous Westminster Kennel Club dog show in New York City. Gambolling Gavin of Galway, a 2½-year-old male owned by Arthur R. and Alicia Whiting, 436 Dalecarlia Drive, took first place in the Sight Hound Division after winning Best of Breed in a field of 24 dogs. To qualify, Gavin won state and regional competitions in July and October. The dog, according to Mr. Whiting, was a wedding gift to his wife.

It was time to go home. The initial sense that I had stumbled on an important obituary with Alicia Whiting's call was quickly fading. The clips all pointed to the fact that Arthur Whiting had led an unremarkable life, and that Alicia had simply inflated her husband's memory.

On my way out, one of the security guards stopped me to hand me a package that had just come in.

"There was a lady in here just a few minutes ago," he said, passing me a thin manila envelope with GORDON HATCH, REPORTER written in large capital letters. "We tried to call you but your line's switched over."

"Did she say anything?" The return address was a personalized sticker, with the Society for the Prevention of Cruelty to Animals logo, of Mr. and Mrs. Arthur R. Whiting.

"Not much," he said. "She wanted to talk to you."

"How old would you say she was?"

"Mid-thirties, blond. She had a big gray coat on. Nice looking."

I thanked him, trying to look casual as I walked out, in case Alicia was just outside. A brisk fall wind had picked up, and the sun was setting just in front of me, about to drop beneath the Cupples Station warehouse, the old freight storage complex on Ninth Avenue. An orange stripe cut across the *Independent's* masthead.

Down the street a docent at the bowling museum was bringing in his signboards and locking up. An elderly couple stood arm and arm at the corner waiting for the light to change.

I turned the envelope over to open it. On the back, Alicia had written "Photo Enclosed." I pictured her husband, his hollow face, thought of her disappointment tomorrow at the tiny obituary: no picture, below the fold. Instead, I slipped the unopened envelope inside my briefcase and headed home.

3

TO PREPARE MYSELF for the night police beat — my next job, I figured — I had bought a scanner that I listened to after coming home from work. It gave me a chance to hear where the homicides were, what neighborhoods were considered unpatrollable, and how long it took police to respond to a call. That evening I had just turned it on and collapsed on my living room couch when the phone rang. Still caught up in the reverie of the day, I almost expected that it was Alicia Whiting calling to make sure I had received the photograph.

"What are you doing home?" my mother asked half accusingly. "You're never home at this hour."

"Research," I said, annoyed.

"What about last night? Where were you? I left a message on your machine and you didn't get back to me."

"I didn't check the machine until late. Too late to call."

"Why didn't you wake me? It's not fair when I don't hear from you."

I turned the scanner's volume to low. "I've been working on an investigative piece," I lied.

"An investigative piece," she repeated, but didn't pursue it. "Did you listen to my message?"

"Yes." I was already growing impatient. "I'm going to see you in a couple of weeks. I thought we talked about it —"

"This time I hope you mean it," she interrupted. "You've promised to make it home before and something always comes up. Expectations have consequences if you can't fulfill them. Today it's me. Tomorrow it could be someone important."

I lay back down on the couch, in no mood for my mother's lecturing.

"I have news about Thea Pierson," she said. "Do you want to hear it?"

"Depends."

"Am I being intrusive again? Is that the problem?"

"What is it you want to tell me?"

"She's moving to St. Louis."

My mother paused, listening for a reaction.

"What do you mean she's moving to St. Louis?"

"She's there as we speak, on a one-year program at SLU Hospital." I heard the strike of a match, her deep inhale. "It's something they do before medical school."

"Really?" I tried not to sound interested.

"Yes, really. She called last night."

"Why St. Louis?" I sat up and turned the scanner off.

"Don't ask me, Gordie. She certainly had a choice. With her record, she could have gone anywhere."

I stretched the phone cord to the bathroom, a few steps away in my tiny apartment, and leaned over the sink to check my reaction up close in the bathroom mirror. Small wrinkles had formed between my eyebrows.

"She still cares," my mother said.

"What does it matter?" I asked.

"Trust me," she said. "She hasn't given up on you."

Thea was born Thuy Linh, one of the few *bui doi*, children of a Vietnamese mother and an American GI, whose father returned to Saigon to claim her. She was four years old when the plane touched down at Columbia Regional Airport. Her father, Daniel

Pierson, had used an old Army officer connection to doctor her birth certificate and change her age to two. He figured Thea could use the extra couple of years. She'd start school late, catch up with the language.

Daniel Pierson was a single man, a third-year doctoral student in public policy, and he must have been lonely when he picked up the phone and dialed an old friend at the Immigration and Naturalization Service. He said he had a daughter by a Vietnamese woman, and what would it take to gain custody? Depends on the woman, his old friend said.

Unlike many new immigrants growing up in America, Thea had no access to her culture and no contact with the country of her birth. The nearest Vietnamese community was on South Grand in St. Louis, an hour and a half away. She said she didn't know about South Grand until she moved there many years later. In Columbia, *bui doi* was just another foreign term.

Not until the sixth grade did she begin to take note of herself. She put pictures on the mirror of other girls in her class — goldilocks, freckle face, and button nose — class pictures with marbled blue backgrounds. She looked at them and back at her reflection, trying to will her stubborn face to do what it couldn't do.

On the Fourth of July, 1979, she returned from the town parade and started a letter to her mother. "My name is Thea Pierson," it began. "You knew me when I was a little girl, and now I would like to know you."

She wrote of friends, school, American things; marching bands and colorful floats, Shriners doing figure eights in mini antique cars; her house, a cat named Ringo who got in through the basement and stayed. It was a long letter that grew by the day, written at school in the margins of books, copied over before bed on a wide-ruled notepad as she lay on her stomach with her feet in the air. It never occurred to her that her mother might not read English.

In the mornings she went to the county library and ripped out pictures of boat people from *Life* magazine, sneaked them into a book, and stapled them to her letter in the girls' room. She read about the Vietnamese living in New Orleans, East Texas, the Mississippi Delta, where it was hot and wet like Vietnam, where shrimp and rice were farmed, wrote about them as if she had been there. By early August, her letter nearly filled the notepad.

Then, a week before Labor Day, around dinnertime, in the middle of another late summer thundershower, her father received a phone call from the same friend at the INS who had originally helped with the papers. Thea's mother had died several months before.

"It was my fault," she told me later. "How could it not be? I started the letter too late."

"But you couldn't have known," I said.

"She was my mother. We had that connection. She was probably waiting for me to write her, expecting it every day," she said. "But I didn't even think about it."

The morning after the phone call, Thea ripped up the letter and put the pieces in a large serving bowl, cut off a lock of her long hair and placed it in the middle. She went to a card shop downtown and bought two fat candles — one red and one yellow, the colors of the South Vietnamese flag — and made a little shrine on her bedside table.

Growing up in Columbia, Thea became a curiosity. She was one of only two Asian students at Columbia Central, and classmates invited her home to show her off, took her to the mall and dressed her up, talked to her as if she were their child. When the novelty wore off, she found herself alone once again. But she was resourceful. She had a breeziness about her, moving with ease from circle to circle, hiding the wounds of abandonment.

I first met her in biology. We dissected a fetal pig together. I didn't expect to like her because I saw who her friends were. They wore Grateful Dead shirts and leather strips around their ankles,

Birkenstocks and cut-off jeans; their heads nodded as they walked. They dropped acid and skipped along the bluffs over the Missouri, sold dope to fraternity boys, stared holes into the tables at Taco Bell.

"I know you," she said, snipping open the bag and filling the air between us with the smell of formaldehyde. "You're the shyest boy in the school."

I got an A on the lab, my first, and found myself saying things to her that I had never told anyone. We went to my favorite deli and bought sandwiches — roast beef on rye with cole slaw and Russian dressing — cut along the Katy Trail to my house where we watched the soaps, drinking sixteen-ounce Dr Peppers with a big bag of Doritos. We must have done that every day for months and into the summer, slumped with our backs against the sofa on the plush orange rug in the living room. I felt my elbow on her waist and I held it there, pressing against her until it seemed dangerous.

She was tall, from her father — we stood eye to eye — long-limbed and willowy. Her light dresses moved with her as she walked, revealing a thin strap, white cotton against her skin, a curve of the hip, a clavicle. I studied her smile, her gestures, the formality with which she spoke, until I could see her mouth and hands in the darkness and hear her voice over the traffic of my mind.

I didn't kiss Thea that first year. She left the circle of Deadheads and spent all of her time with me. She stayed over at night, sometimes for the whole weekend when her father was away, sleeping in my bed while I lay on the living room couch with her image flickering above me as I drifted off.

We talked about my father and her mother and growing up without them. I told her about Wichita, Dallas, Chicago, far-flung places I knew from my mother's stories and a few vague memories. She said one day she'd like to go to Vietnam and look for her relatives.

"When?" I asked.

"When I'm ready," she said.

And that was all. She knew next to nothing about her mother, had no photographs or memories of her mother's face, and would not have known where to start had she wanted to invent a life for her. Daniel Pierson would say only that Thea's mother lived in Saigon, that he knew her briefly, that his memory had been scattered by the war. She gave Thea up for adoption in 1972, the same year my father died.

"So both of us are orphans," Thea told me.

I had never thought of myself as an orphan before, but coming from Thea it sounded true. We were orphans. That was our bond.

When we graduated high school, she took a summer job as a candy striper at the university hospital while I worked as a copy boy for the *Columbia Pioneer*. Soon, with her father running a conference in D.C., she was spending nearly every night at our house, and life at 102 La Grange was too good to be true: Thea and I under the same roof, making hamburgers and homemade chicken fingers and the most delightfully unhealthy meals, going to Cajun Stella's for oysters on the half shell and blues at the amphitheater.

My mother, for the most part, made a great effort to stay out of our way. Early in the summer, though, she couldn't help but meddle. She cooked us casseroles, stayed up late, actually bought board games for the three of us to play. She said there were shades of her relationship with my father in my friendship with Thea, and went so far as to make copies of some old Western Union telegrams from one of my father's tours in the Navy. She left them on my desk so I could glimpse their own great love affair. For years I kept "AT SEA WITHOUT YOU," wired by my father in 1960 from the Midway Islands, in a tiny compartment in my wallet.

As the summer wore on, my mother got the sense that we'd rather be alone and she disappeared, communicating mostly by notes and long, friendly messages on the answering machine. She worked all day and volunteered nights for the university's Gilbert and Sullivan Society, helping with costumes (her mother had been a seamstress in Greencastle, Indiana) for a summer-stock run of *H.M.S. Pinafore.*

Meanwhile, Thea's touch was coloring the house. Each day I'd come back from work to find something new — a polished candlestick, a linen lampshade where a plastic one had been, plants in all the windows: African violets and daisies in the living room, begonias and English ivy in a box by the kitchen sink, an amaryllis on the sill in my mother's room. I found a hanging fuchsia in the bathroom one day and a tree with red peppers sitting on my desk.

With Thea around I became aware of the dreariness of our house: walls and moldings in need of paint, heavy gray curtains that blocked out the light, yellowing antimacassars on the living room couch, chairs that needed recaning. As clean as she kept it, my mother was content with the same old decor. Things I had once considered cheerful, like the orange rug she had installed when we moved in and the Bavarian cuckoo clock that no longer worked, now seemed grim.

One Saturday in August, a day after we had gone out with my mother for her birthday, Thea left the house to do an early round at the hospital. I had the day off and spent the morning in the garage making room for back copies of the *Washington Post,* a new addition to my newspaper collection. At lunchtime I walked to the deli and thought I might order a roast beef on rye with cole slaw and Russian dressing but, remembering the sanctity of that sandwich, to be shared with Thea only, decided on a turkey and onion instead. Rather than cutting through the Katy Trail, I took the long route home, along Maple to Eighth, then down to Stadium and La Grange.

At the corner of Eighth and Maple was a small nursery called College Gardens dealing mostly in house plants. I bought my mother a ficus there once, which died the summer we went to Florida when our boarders neglected to water it.

It must have been the red and white of her candy striper uniform that caught my eye. Leaning on her elbows with her chin in her hands, moving her head from side to side coquettishly, at the window of a little shack by the greenhouse, was Thea. She was turned in the direction of a ponytailed garden clerk, who moved busily about in his hut. I crossed the street and ducked behind a car.

He was tall and blond with a scruffy beard and a tie-dyed shirt under his green garden smock. I couldn't hear what he was saying but it must have been amusing because Thea was laughing, clapping her hands together. When a customer stepped up to the shack hauling a rubber tree, Thea straightened and began to turn.

I walked hastily down Eighth, my mind a blank. At home I went directly to bed.

My mother came into the room sometime after six.

"Thea called about a half hour ago," she said. "She won't be back for dinner."

All night I waited for Thea to come home. When my mother turned in, I sat on the living room couch with the lights off waiting for the sound of a key in the door. A few times that summer Thea had slept at her own house to watch over things for her father. Now I knew why.

I went to the bedroom and buried my nose in the pillow where she had slept all summer. It smelled like Florida.

The night before at my mother's birthday dinner, Thea had said that with us she had finally found a sense of belonging. Now I imagined the garden clerk with his ponytail and tie-dyed shirt, leaning down and kissing Thea full on the lips, taking her hand, whisking her away.

At four in the morning, still awake, I went outside and sat on the front steps, where I fell asleep in the humid August air until the thump of the Sunday paper woke me and sent me back to my bedroom.

Not until noon, just as I was getting up, did Thea finally call, inviting my mother and me to lunch downtown.

"I'm sorry we missed each other last night," she began to say.

"Mother's busy," I said. "I'll meet you at Booche's in an hour."

Booche's was an old pool hall with warped cue sticks and excellent hamburgers just off the main drag on Ninth Street.

"Should we get a table?" she asked, hugging me as I walked in.

The pool hall was frigid, and I was sweating from the walk over. They always kept the a.c. too high in the summertime.

"Where were you last night?"

We took our places at the window seat. She looked at me steadily.

"I was out with a friend."

"What kind of a friend?" The nerves tightened my throat.

"Someone I knew from before," she said. "He used to live here but he moved away when his parents got divorced." She looked into her lap, where her hands were folded. "I saw him at Schnucks about a month ago and he told me he was working at the nursery."

"So that's where you've been getting the plants, isn't it?" I shifted in my seat.

She nodded yes, matter-of-factly. "Stuart gave them to me as gifts," she said, as if there were nothing wrong. "Every time I stopped by, he wouldn't let me leave unless I took something. I told him about you and Lorraine and the house and everything. He said it was his pleasure."

"His pleasure?" I raised my voice. "Stealing from his workplace!"

"It's his father's nursery," she said, as if that explained everything. "All those plants are his to give away."

I felt myself slouching.

"You'd like him a lot," she said.

"Oh, sure. I imagine I'd really like him."

"No, I mean it, Gordie. The three of us should go out sometime."

As the burgers arrived I excused myself, saying there was something I needed to do. I walked out of Booche's and over to Fifth, crossed Stadium, then four more blocks to my house. My mother was gone but the car was still there, so I loaded up the Gremlin with Thea's plants and drove them over to the nursery. I took them out one by one — begonias, violets, daisies and ivy, the amaryllis, the pepper tree, the hanging fuchsia, the orange tree, and the camellia — and left them at the little hut by the greenhouse.

"Do you have an employee here named Stuart?" I asked another ponytailed garden clerk who had come over to assist me. "Tell him I have no use for these plants."

For the rest of the summer I ignored Thea's calls. My mother's plea for me to be reasonable had no effect, and as college began, all of my energies focused on proving myself. I would be a student and after that a journalist. Nothing else mattered.

Clearly I had not been ready for the complexities of love, but one day I knew I would find the pure perfect woman, and I'd show Thea Pierson what a mistake she had made.

"Thea would like to call you," my mother said, bringing me back to the present.

"Why's that?" I was pacing. "I haven't spoken with her in four years."

"I don't know, Gordie. She still talks about you. She says she'll never understand what happened. One day you were the best of friends. The next you were leaving the house any time she stopped by."

I had never given my mother a proper explanation. I'd simply said we'd had a sudden falling out. "It's probably for the best anyway. I need to concentrate on more important things."

But my mother had kept in touch with her, mostly by mail, when Thea went off to Brown University and then to summer internships at NIH in D.C. and the Houston Medical Center. She'd leave Thea's letters open on the dinette table hoping that I'd read them. And I did, of course, but there was never any mention of boyfriends and only good-natured questions about me.

Every once in a while I'd see Thea's father, around campus or eating alone at a restaurant bar, his face buried in the *Nation* or the *New York Review of Books*, and inevitably I'd think about her.

"She doesn't know anyone in St. Louis," my mother said. "I think it would be decent of you to make her feel welcome."

"I don't know anyone in St. Louis either." I thought of Alicia Whiting, also alone, but in her well-appointed house, her show dog curled at her feet.

"That's not the point, Gordie. She's a stranger in the city, and a woman. Certain things you have to do for the sake of decency."

"I'm extremely busy," I said. "It's not like I work a nine-to-five job."

"Well, I've given her your number," my mother said, and with that she hung up.

4

I CAME IN TO WORK early Sunday morning feeling out of balance. I needed to clear my head, so I sat at my desk and read the *New York Times* and the *Independent* from cover to cover, concentrating on every detail, as if trying to commit the stories to memory.

Nineteen eighty-nine had become the year of foreign news. The civil war in Nicaragua was over, the Soviets were out of Afghanistan, Solidarity had been legalized in Poland, paving the way for democratic reform. Hungary had moved to socialism without a show of force from the Soviet government. And for six weeks in May and early June, China had seemed headed for reform as well.

Part of me wished all the upheaval could be delayed. Why was the world changing so rapidly at *this* moment, while I still labored in the clattering outpost of Obits? I didn't doubt that I would still be touched by history, but 1989, as it was shaping up, felt like an opportunity passing me by. I wanted to be in Eastern Europe — I daydreamed of reporting from the next great flashpoint — but I doubted that even my father would have picked up the Sunday paper and said *That's where the story is* and hopped the next plane to Prague.

I was an obituary writer. My job was taking the measure of people's lives. I wanted to move on from this assignment but had to believe that it was not unimportant, even if obituary writing, when

I came to think of it, was something of journalism's opposite: instead of going out to find the story, the story comes to you.

I decided my next three advancers would be the dictators still in power in Eastern Europe: Zhivkov in Bulgaria, Ceausescu in Romania, Honecker in East Germany. One was certain to die in a coup. They were old anyway. The unrest would be too much for their black hearts to take.

I was working on Erich Honecker's obit when Dick Ritger walked in.

"What are you doing here, Hatch?" he asked, talking through his teeth.

"Just looking at the final." I slid the newspaper over my research books and closed the personal file on my computer.

"You're off today, aren't you?"

"Just getting organized."

Ritger threw down his shoulder bag, picking some coins out of a glass on his desk, counting them in his palm.

"It's a nice day outside. You make me nervous coming in here when it's so nice outside."

I smiled uncomfortably.

"I'm getting a coffee. Need something from the cafeteria?"

"No." I hesitated, taken aback by his gesture of kindness. "Thanks, though."

He pulled a file off his desk, slid it among the inserts in his newspaper, and made his way to the stairwell.

Ritger's coffee break extended well into the morning, allowing me to linger more than I should have on a particular historical abstract about President Kennedy's visit to Germany in the summer of 1963. This was the famous visit of *"Ich bin ein Berliner,"* when Kennedy mounted a platform at Checkpoint Charlie, surveying the bleak city of East Berlin, broken and gray on the other side of the wall.

"There are some who say that communism is the wave of the future," he had said. "Let them come to Berlin."

Ritger returned to the desk around eleven o'clock as the phone was ringing.

"I'll get that." He picked it up, a sour look crossing his face as he handed me the phone.

"For you."

It was Alicia Whiting. "I wanted to apologize for yesterday," she began. "I've been quite out of sorts since my husband's death."

"It's okay," I said.

"It happened so suddenly, you can't imagine. I can hardly sit still. I keep going to the window, as if it's permanently five o'clock and he'll be pulling into the driveway any minute."

"I understand."

"Did you get the picture that I left for you?"

I opened my briefcase and pulled out the still unopened envelope.

"I did." I tore it open now to see the five-by-seven head shot of Arthur Whiting. "He's very distinguished looking."

The obituary this morning had looked so meager in the lower right-hand corner of metro page D-7 that I had turned the page without reading it, moving quickly to another section. I worried that she would be disappointed with five dispassionate inches, having spent so much time on the phone with me.

"I'm sorry about the page," I said. "Your call came so late and everything. At least we got it in before the funeral."

"There's so much more I have to tell you about Arthur," she said.

Perhaps she wasn't hearing me. "About the obituary this morning — I hope you understand why we didn't run the picture." I enunciated clearly.

"Oh, I understand," she said. "You have deadlines, and we didn't make it in time. You did what you could under the circumstances, and I appreciate it."

Of course no amount of forethought would have gotten Arthur Whiting more than a couple of paragraphs, but I wasn't about to tell her that.

"I want to show you a few things," she said over what sounded like running water. "Today's Sunday. Maybe you'll be free this afternoon?"

In the year since I'd moved to St. Louis, the only woman to call me besides my mother and the long-distance and credit-card companies was a sweet-sounding girl from the St. Louis Symphony, who stayed on the line for nearly half an hour until her supervisor made her cut me off. She called at my apartment, waking me from a nap, and I was too tired at the time to rush her off the phone. I had to admit that I liked the feeling of coming out of sleep to a woman's voice.

"I don't usually meet with people." I hesitated. "I'm an obituary writer. I do all of my work on the phone."

"I won't take much of your time, but I think Arthur's story will interest you . . . The least I owe you is a cup of coffee for rambling on yesterday."

"I'm not sure —" My mind was turning over excuses.

"You see," she interrupted. "I have an idea for a feature. There's much more to my husband than it might seem on the surface. People aren't just raw facts and data, you know. Some of the most interesting things happen to ordinary people."

I thought of the *Washington Post*'s obituary page, how under each name, in bold print, there was a subheading for occupation. I had never much liked the *Post*'s policy, as if individuals were indistinguishable from their jobs.

"They make you work on Sundays?" Alicia asked, as if this had just occurred to her.

In the background I could hear her turn off the water, take a couple of steps, and sit down with the phone. After a moment, she said, "Maybe you should describe yourself."

"What do you mean?"

"If I'm going to meet you, I need to know what you look like."

I wasn't sure how to respond, so I went ahead and told her that I was thin, but not from lack of appetite, with brown hair, and that my ears were somewhat prominent, which they were, since I had just been to the barber.

"Are you tall?"

"Not really. Five eight, five nine."

I'd never taken much interest in my appearance until I finished growing, when my mother began to point out that I looked like a slighter version of my father. "He had tremendous presence," she liked to say. "He could light up a room."

I told Alicia I had a long face.

"I like long faces on men," she said. "Fred Astaire had a long face and I'm very fond of him."

Fred Astaire had been my mother's girlhood crush. She used to make my father jealous by bringing up his name, closing her eyes, and dancing around the room with her arms pulled back. Years later she bought tapes of his musical classics — *Swing Time, Royal Wedding, Easter Parade* — which Thea and I used to watch.

"That's funny," I said, thinking out loud, a warm wave running down my back. I held the picture of Arthur Whiting in my hand: a sharply handsome man in a striped tie, looking more the banker here than in the newspaper shot, stiffly posed.

"How about we meet at Union Station, at the top of the marble staircase," she suggested. "The one that goes up to that magnificent room.

"Two o'clock?" she pressed.

I hesitated, then figured that meeting her was at least the decent thing to do. "Two's fine."

"I'll be wearing a burgundy dress."

They were strange parting words — almost as if I had just agreed to something more like a blind date.

After her call I couldn't concentrate. I tried returning to the Honecker obit, but my mind kept wandering back to Alicia's voice. I had to admit that I was curious to meet her, not that I expected there was any kind of story. More than likely, she wanted to see her husband memorialized — an article, a picture, something to show for Arthur Whiting's life.

But, then, perhaps there was a story. "Interesting things happen to ordinary people," she had said, and certainly this was true. How could my father have known that the President would be shot in Dallas the next day? His instincts told him, *Go.*

I was leaning back in my chair, my feet kicked up next to the computer, when Ritger shouted "Hatch" from somewhere nearby. I picked up the newspaper and pretended to read it.

"Hatch," he said again. "Bette Davis just died and Jim wants it on the keybox. Call AP and get us a preview."

I sat there a long moment, the paper resting on my chest.

Bette Davis was one of my advancers.

I said nothing to Ritger. The beauty of my advancer file was that I had kept it a secret. Seventy-nine obituaries, stashed like gold in a hidden vault. I could almost sense my father's hand aligning the stars to make this happen, could feel the actual shiver of approaching destiny. I pictured Jim St. John tomorrow morning when I'd hand him each one — Nixon, Ford, Carter, Reagan, and so on and so on, the sudden life in his face as he recognized the prospect, the enormous talent standing before him.

I tore off the AP bulletin — BETTE DAVIS DIES — from one of the wire machines by the entrance to the newsroom, checked the article for cause of death, pulled the Davis advancer out of my personal file, and plugged in the updates. My lead began:

> Bette Davis, who hoped her epitaph would read "She Did It the Hard Way," died today of rodentoid cancer at Cedars-Sinai Medical Center in Los Angeles at the age of 81. Ms. Davis, whose 101 feature films included Best Actress Academy Awards for "Dangerous" in 1935 and "Jezebel" in 1938, is likely to be remembered as the first modern woman of the silver screen. Emotionally intense, fiercely independent, outspoken and in charge, she created a new prototype for the Hollywood heroine.

I called AP in Chicago to find out how many inches their obituary would be — twenty-four — and trimmed my own so the length of mine would be consistent with theirs. In the photo lab, I looked through movie stills of Bette Davis as they came across the AP photo machine. For the front page I picked a close-up from *The Private Lives of Elizabeth and Essex,* with Davis playing an aging Queen Elizabeth. The movie was made in 1939, the same year she turned down the role of Scarlett O'Hara in *Gone with the Wind.* In the picture, she's thirty-one made up to look sixty. It was eerie how similarly she had aged in real life.

In the midst of my excitement, I felt a genuine sadness for Bette Davis, as if she were someone I used to know but hadn't seen in years, or a memorable acquaintance who had confided a personal story. I remembered writing her obituary back in April, when I had first heard that she was sick. She had been my forty-second advancer. Forty-two, I noted — my new lucky number.

When I had walked the photograph to the layout desk and read through the obituary word by word, thrilled at how genuinely good it was, I made one final change: on the line above the obit, which before always used to read, *Reprinted courtesy of the Associated Press,* I wrote, *Courtesy of St. Louis Independent staff reports.*

I slipped a printout into my briefcase for safekeeping and sent the computer file OBIT/DAVIS to the copy desk for proofreading.

5

THE WALK TO Union Station calmed me. It was a warm fall day, bright and still, and I moved quickly, as if on assignment. I knew later that I'd remember each detail of the past hour — the sound of Ritger's voice, the shape of the words BETTE DAVIS DIES, her hair plucked back in ringlets for the role of Queen Elizabeth — but for now, outside, the day dissolved into a general happiness.

At Walnut and Tenth I hit traffic: groups passing me on the sidewalk, some in lederhosen and funny German hats; a flatbed truck idling at an intersection with a band in the back playing oompah music; lines of cars heading for the Oktoberfest down by the river. I sensed people watching me as I crossed the street, wondering who I was and where I was going, so crisp and confident, moving against the tide.

Beyond Kiel Auditorium, the sky opened to a spired clock tower, once the façade of the largest train station in the world, now all shops and restaurants. I pushed open the heavy doors at the front entrance and fell in with the crowd.

Under the high open ceiling of red girders and pipes, the lacquered brick floor was alive with activity. More German music was playing from dozens of movable kiosks. The midday sun filtered through the skylights, making patterns on people's faces as they passed, and I imagined myself weaving through the charged streets of Prague on my way to see Havel for an exclusive interview. He'd invite me in, then talk of his essays, his plays, of Jefferson and the framers of the Constitution, the role of intellectuals in a new democracy. A pool photographer would get our picture, Havel and I shaking hands, leaning across a standing ashtray in a large bare room. And I would feel, in that instant with the leader of the revolution beside me, my life converging with my father's.

From the banister of the magnificent waiting room at Union Station, upstairs from all the shops and restaurants, I was watching the marble staircase when she finally appeared, a small woman in a long burgundy dress covered by a loose-fitting cardigan.

"Gordon Hatch," she said as she came up the stairs. "I'm late. I'm always late." She took my hand in her cold fingers. "I'm glad you came."

Up close, she looked even younger than I had imagined. Her soft features seemed to fit her voice, and I was startled by her loveliness. She had gray eyes flecked with yellow, blond hair, lighter at the ends, in a kind of natural disarray; and though she was petite, she had a luminescent quality that took up space.

"I'm sorry. The traffic was terrible," she said. Her lips settled into a frown, hinting at a sad prettiness.

I put my hands in my pockets, suddenly feeling self-conscious. "They're having a festival downtown," I said stupidly.

"The funeral is on Tuesday." She settled into a chair under an old-fashioned floor lamp. "It's at eleven o'clock. Don't feel you have to bring anything."

Her eyebrows lifted slightly as if to say, *You'll be there, of course.*

I nodded, vaguely considering my Tuesday routine.

"A lot of people wonder how Arthur and I ever got together," she began. "We must have seemed very different. I was a painter and he worked at a bank. I read metaphysical books and he was overly attached to the stock pages."

Sitting in a chair across from her, I pulled a notepad out of my back pocket and pretended to take notes.

"Arthur was ten years older, and if I hadn't come along he probably never would have married," she said. "He kept charts on his computer where he recorded his entire day in half-hour blocks. 'Watched Tom Brokaw,' he'd write next to six P.M., or 'Gavin to Battery Park.' That's our dog," she said to me, as if in confidence. "I used to make fun of him for it. 'Enquiring minds want to know,' he'd joke."

I nodded. It was a relief to have the pen and paper and not have to find something to do with my hands.

"I thought it was sweet the way he'd write memos to himself all day," she said, "then sit at the computer filling out his spreadsheet. He got so intense. He couldn't be bothered when he was filling out that grid."

She continued in this way, speaking with fondness of Arthur's little quirks, painting the portrait of an ordinary, if obsessive, man. She was right about what an unlikely pair they made.

She wore hoop earrings, big gold hoops that waved when she shook her head, and bangles on her wrists and silver rings. There was something about her eyebrows, too: they were darker than her hair and groomed into perfect narrow arches in a way that made the flesh above her eyes look soft as pillows, as though she had just awoken from a light nap.

"We met at a time in my life when I was really looking for order. It's just like me to go overboard," she said. "He offered the complete antithesis to the life I had been living, and we were generally very happy." She laughed, a high-pitched, almost mischievous giggle. "He told me that I was his creative side, his adopted imagination. I signed him up for a ceramics class, but that was pushing it too far."

I was half listening, half trying to understand why she had invited me into their private world. I felt more like a grief counselor than a reporter.

"I'm such a wreck," she said, combing her hair behind her ears with her fingers. "All I do is laugh or cry."

I'm usually a guarded person, the type who assesses everything from a distance, where I can make my judgments and approach with expectations. I find it minimizes the chances of humiliation. With Alicia, however, I was on my heels from the start.

"Well, this is really what I wanted to talk to you about," she said, as though the rest had all been meaningless matter. She pulled a thick manila envelope from her floral handbag and shook its contents onto the bench: clips, most of them recent, torn from Chicago, Denver, and Oklahoma City newspapers, and several from the *Independent*.

"I collect them," she explained.

I sifted through the odd assortment of articles, reading the captions and leads, aware of Alicia's watching me.

There was one about a fireman who had glued bottle caps over every inch of his house, another about a barber who had woven a giant ball of hair from sweepings of his floor; there was the wife of the mayor of Enid, Oklahoma, who had opened a museum for her five thousand dolls, and a Denver lawyer who after losing a case hiked from the Rockies to Newfoundland.

"I want you to do a feature," Alicia said.

"A feature? What about?" I couldn't imagine what it might be, and yet I was beginning to feel I should do anything for this young widow, whose fractured life had been thrown in my direction.

"On Arthur." She smiled.

The ink-and-chemical smell of the newspaper clips had calmed me, and I began to feel a kind of confidence that comes, even to the shyest people, when grounded once again in the familiar. I was the journalist, an authority, and I wanted to impress her. "Are you sure there's a story?" I pointed to the clips: the barber and the bottle caps, the doll collection, the cross-country hike. "These things don't happen every day. In every feature there has to be a hook."

Alicia's face drained of expression. I could almost feel her drifting away. "You need a story," I said solicitously. "If you've got a story, we can really go somewhere."

I felt an unexplainable urge to touch her shoulder where the cardigan was slipping down, to lift the lock of hair that had strayed across her face and place it back behind her ear, to take her hand and turn the silver rings around her fingers.

"I have a story," Alicia said, seeming herself again. "You'll have to let me think about it some more, but I do have a story."

She talked then about the funeral arrangements. She had to drive out to the country on Monday to pick up her brother-in-law, Joe. "He's kind of funny, you'll see. He's not allowed to have a car." And Arthur's sister could be stopping by at any time. Between now and Tuesday she had a hundred things to get ready.

"Who knew funerals could be so stressful? Besides, I'm not very good with big groups. I prefer one on one," she said. "I used to tell Arthur that I knew we could be happy, just the two of us, out on a big ranch in Montana, with nobody around but the dogs. In Montana, they speak of land in units, not acres. Isn't that funny? Just us and the biggest blue sky."

Thea had told me she wanted to live by the ocean. We'd have a wood-burning stove in a camp house up high on the rocks over the Pacific, somewhere in Oregon or northern California, near a town of carpenters and potters and fishermen, real people who smelled of their work.

Alicia stood up, stuffing the clips back into the envelope.

"Well, goodbye Gordon Hatch. It's been nice meeting you." She smiled. "I'll call you about Tuesday. I need you to be there."

6

I WAS STANDING at a long traffic light, the bright sun warming my scalp, when I decided I couldn't wait to see my Bette Davis obit on the page. Tomorrow morning I'd call Alicia to tell her who wrote it. She'd read her favorite parts aloud and say what a wonderful writer I was. Where did I get such a talent? She would tear the obit out, slipping it among the clips in her thick manila envelope.

By now, at four o'clock, the copy desk would have written a headline and caption and sent the obit downstairs to the composing room. A composing technician would be pasting the typeset copy onto a drafting board, making page proofs for editors to review, sending the board along a conveyer belt for platemaking. St. John would see a proof within the next half hour, and I wanted to be nearby for his reaction.

A new guard was working at the security desk.

"How are ya?" I said, flashing my ID. "Gordon Hatch. I'm a reporter up in the newsroom."

He had a look of distrust as I shook his hand.

Jessie Tennant, one of the metro columnists, joined me in the elevator. A thin woman with chestnut skin who dressed as if every day were Easter, she wrote about neighborhoods, mostly in East St. Louis. Her husband was a press operator and her son worked in Distribution, so she usually kept night hours. Editors were afraid of her. Not merely for her strong opinions. She was elusive: formal on the phone, with the tidiest desk in the newsroom, hers the only column that ran without a mug shot. I didn't realize, arriving early each morning to work on my advancers, that seeing Jessie Tennant in her bright pinks and yellows was an uncommon privilege.

I punched 5 for composing and 6 for the newsroom. "Isn't this a little early for you?" I asked, feeling a rare gregariousness overcome me.

As often as I had seen her, we'd never spoken. She always looked absorbed in her work and over time I'd gotten used to it, she and I alone in the newsroom at eight-fifteen in the morning, not bothering to introduce ourselves.

"They're having a special meeting on minority hiring," she said. "They wanted me to be there."

"I'm Gordon Hatch."

"I know who you are," she said as I got off on 5.

At the obituary page drafting board, I admired a proof copy of the Davis obit. SCREEN LEGEND BETTE DAVIS DEAD AT 81, the headline read. Under her picture, the copy editor had written *Bette Davis as Queen Elizabeth, 1939.*

I found Greg DePaul, the composing room foreman, and asked him if the page was on its way to be plated, and he made a tasteless joke about Bette Davis's being "primped, pressed, and put on rollers."

"You know who wrote it?" I asked.

"I just move the pages," he said with practiced boredom.

"I wrote it," I told him. "I've got a huge advancer file in my computer, and I've had this thing lying around since April. As far as we're concerned, the old lady's been dead for six months."

Climbing the stairs one floor to the newsroom, I regretted this last comment. I always feel guilty saying what I don't believe, particularly for the cause of male camaraderie.

The newsroom was quiet, typical for a late Sunday afternoon.

From the east wall I could see editors and columnists from various sections streaming into the conference room. In the distance I saw Ritger with a proof sheet, and stepped up my pace.

Passing the photo lab and the research library, I walked by the open conference room door, my hands in my pockets, feigning casualness. St. John stood in the doorway wearing a silver and blue galaxy tie.

"You want to come in here a minute," he said, motioning with his hands. He had large hands for a man his size.

Ritger was sitting in one of the chairs along the perimeter, not bothering to look up at me. On the dark-paneled wall behind him hung the lithograph of Joseph Charless and his hand-operated press and five somber portraits of the *Independent*'s publishers since 1945.

Jessie Tennant sat near the head of the table, next to St. John's empty chair. On the long glass table lay a proof of metro page D-7, with the headline across the top: SCREEN LEGEND BETTE DAVIS DEAD AT 81.

More than a dozen people were there: Jason Haas from Business, Matt Mankowski from Sports, Beatriz Acevedo from the editorial page, Doug Greiff from Entertainment, city desk editor J. B. Loveland, and Gloria De Angelis, who ran special assignments for Metro. Several columnists, among them Hannah Greene and Ben Richards, sat in a row between Jessie Tennant and the young reporter Marshall Holman, who had left my slot to work the night police beat.

I remained standing near the middle of the room. Jim St. John closed the door and took his seat at the head of the conference table.

I moved forward as if I were about to say something, but somehow my mind was a blank. I had been expecting congratulations, an instant promotion, a collegial embrace, but there was an unsettling feeling about the room.

"Before you get started, Hatch, let me tell you a little story." St. John leaned forward, putting his elbows on the table. "I'll make it quick. I don't need to remind you that we work on a deadline.

"Last night, I went to my son's school — he's in the seventh grade at Kirkwood — and something happened that I think has a lesson in it."

People around me shifted in their chairs.

"They were putting on a play — *King Arthur and the Knights of the Round Table* — and Jimmy was in the lead," St. John said. "A pretty big deal for him, since a lot of kids tried out for King Arthur and he ended up getting it."

St. John's voice was oppressive. I wondered where this was going. Was I supposed to congratulate him on his son's success?

"This one kid in the play didn't have any lines — he was a minor knight — but he was putting everything into it, like *he* had pulled the sword from the stone."

I fixed my eyes to a spot above St. John's head where an old page plate of the Mississippi's worst flood hung on the wall, with the banner headline AN OLD MAN RISES.

"So it's the wedding scene with Guinevere. She and Jimmy say their vows and give each other a kiss, and the knights swear never to fight in an unjust cause and always to protect damsels and widows, then everyone leaves except Jimmy and Guinevere and this one kid."

St. John seemed to be enjoying himself. I could feel him looking around the room.

"Never mind that in the scene before, the kid fell off the stage in a lance fight. Now he's right in the middle of the big romantic moment between the king and queen, and he's too busy swishing his goddamn sword around to notice that all the other knights have cleared the stage."

The room had fallen completely still.

"What do you make of that story, Hatch?"

I shook my head. What did he want me to say? That his son must have been upset having his big moment stolen? That chivalry is dead? That when it comes to women, men do the craziest things?

I scanned the room for a potential savior and came up empty. Everyone was looking down, with the exception, I'd later remember, of Jessie Tennant, who was eyeing St. John. My face felt hot.

"I'll tell you what to make of that story." St. John sat up. "Everyone's got a role to play in this life, and if you stick to your role, it'll all work out."

He picked up the Davis obit as if it were a dead mouse.

"If I had wanted the obituary desk to have an advancer file, I'd have asked for it a long time ago."

He dropped the page proof in front of me and got up to open the door.

As a boy, I used to imagine that the news of the world happened just around the corner: dictators lived up the street, planes were shot from the sky as I slept, anyone in a raincoat could be a foreign agent.

One sunny Wednesday when I was in fourth grade, I had been walking behind a young dark-haired woman in big purple sunglasses and a long black coat heading toward Boone County Savings Bank. As she turned, I saw under the shadow of her black beret what I was sure was the slender nose and subverted stare of Patty Hearst. I knew her face, her walk, the smiling girl from childhood photos that I'd seen in the newspapers. I imagined her captors, dark and crazy, in an idling van. By turning her in, I had thought I might save her.

I ran the three blocks up to Elm and west a block to the precinct station, where I stopped a policeman on his way out the door.

"Patty Hearst is robbing a bank!" I shouted.

"Is that a fact?" He cocked his head and frowned, folding his large forearms high on his chest. "And what bank would that be?"

"Boone," I said, nearly out of breath.

He put a hand on my shoulder, not reassuringly, and asked me how old I was.

"Nine," I told him. "I saw her walk in. I followed her all the way from the card shop."

"And what *time* is it?" the officer asked, leading me inside the station to a room where more policemen were sitting around finishing lunch.

"The kidnappers are there too. I didn't see them, but I know they're there. I bet they're in the alley waiting for her."

The officer leaned over me. He had a thick red mustache and a cleft chin, poorly shaved. "Let's not play games. I asked you what *time* it is."

"One o'clock," I guessed.

"It's two in the afternoon, young man. Where're you supposed to be at two o'clock on a Wednesday afternoon? Aren't you supposed to *be* somewhere right now?"

It was a school holiday. I had every reason to be wandering around downtown, but as the officer's face darkened and I realized that he didn't believe me, I grew quiet. He asked if I knew what the word "truant" meant, said I better not have any pals up the street hoping to make a fool of a police officer. "Did you ever wonder what it's like to spend the night in jail?" he asked.

When it was over, when he had sat me down at his black metal desk and called my mother, sending her into hysterics, when he had humiliated me in front of his grinning cop friends, I promised myself never again would I assume that anyone else knew good from bad, right from wrong, virtue from corruption. He had had Patty Hearst within his grasp — and had let her go. I knew. From now on, that would have to be enough.

I sat at my desk, the lead-removing fan clattering away, surrounding me in white noise. I crumpled up the Davis obituary and hit the speed-dial button for AP Chicago. In a few minutes the AP article appeared on my screen. The length had not changed — still twenty-four inches. I called Layout to say we were running a correction on text but that the picture and the page layout would not be affected. I called the copy desk to promise them a new version just as soon as I had it, and I read through the AP obit word by word, struggling to concentrate.

AP's obituary was a mere catalogue of Bette Davis films and a few quotes from critics and old-timers that did nothing to capture the world-weariness and wisdom of the great actress. None of her good lines was mentioned — "I'd like to kiss ya, but I just washed my hair." And the article dwelt more on her mannerisms — the batting eyes, the sweeping gestures — than it did on her role in Hollywood history.

Above the obit, as I had done countless times before, I typed, *Reprinted courtesy of the Associated Press.*

Later, around five-thirty, after avoiding Greg DePaul in the composing room, where I checked and double-checked that the AP obit, not mine, would be running in the first and all subsequent editions, I stopped by St. John's office.

I had planned to leave a note, but he was there. His diversity meeting must have ended early.

"I've moved the Davis obit from AP," I said. "The length is the same, and it looks fine on the page."

St. John had a so-you've-learned-your-lesson smirk on his face.

"Good, Hatch," he said. "Good."

"Do you need me to stay around? It's my day off," I reminded him.

"Nope," he said with a bottom-lip smile and a backhand motion toward the door.

I walked out, turning left for the elevators, and made my way home, counting off the names in my head, like a passenger list from an airline disaster, of seventy-nine advancers that would never make it to print.

7

SUNDAY NIGHT and all day Monday I waited for Alicia to call. I checked the machine from work, then the switchboard from home every hour, my mood shifting between angry and resigned. One minute I'd feel determined to prove St. John wrong; the next I'd wonder whether I'd blown my career.

My mother often talked about one of my father's early trials. He was posted in Dallas in the winter of '64, still working for the *Kansan* but beginning to outgrow the small paper. His editor in Wichita, out of jealousy or in a misbegotten attempt to try to hold on to him, kept reining him in, killing any material that lacked a clear, identifiable source. My father had befriended a Dallas police captain who was feeding him stories about Oswald's connections with the Communists and his links to Jack Ruby days ahead of any of the other papers, but the Wichita editor held fast to a policy that no stories would appear that didn't name names.

"Today such a policy would be preposterous," my mother would say. "What if Ben Bradlee had told Woodward and Bernstein that he wouldn't run the Watergate stories until Woodward revealed the identity of Deep Throat? Your father wasn't about to break the most sacred law of journalism and betray a source."

My parents had argued over what to do. My mother encouraged my father to leave the *Kansan,* but my father had been born and raised in Wichita and felt a strong loyalty to his hometown paper, particularly since he had put its name on the journalistic map. But in the end, my mother convinced him to take the Dallas bureau job with the *Chicago Tribune,* which had been coveting him for months.

Compared to my father's, my own troubles seemed insignificant.

By late Monday night, Alicia still hadn't called. I busied myself with making dinner — shredded wheat doused in blueberry yogurt — and cleaning the apartment. I swept the floor and wiped down the kitchen counter, gathered up the Sunday newspaper and put it in the closet along with the others. Finally I turned the scanner on low and listened awhile. Someone had run his car off I-64 and firefighters were cutting him out. A row house had caught fire in Dogtown but apparently no one had been home. In between images of mayhem, pictures of Alicia kept appearing in my mind, her slimness, the way she covered her mouth when she laughed, the sound of her bangles sliding down her arms, clinking together as she combed back her hair.

I turned on the news and watched street scenes from Czechoslovakia — swarms of students in Wenceslas Square demonstrating peacefully. I called the switchboard at work one last time, left a message for Ritger that something had come up and I wouldn't be in until the afternoon, then fell asleep on the couch with the lights still on.

On Tuesday morning, I checked Arthur Whiting's death notice for the location of his funeral. Just as I was leaving the apartment for the funeral home, the phone rang.

"Is that you, Gordie?"

I needed a second to recognize the voice.

"I got the number from your mom." It was Thea, sounding far away. "I know you hate to be bothered at work, so I called here."

"Oh, it's fine, I'm always happy to hear from you," I said, my voice pulling back in a way that must have let her know that I was headed out the door. "So how have you been?"

"Is this a bad time?" she asked.

"No. No. It's perfectly okay."

I heard an echo over the phone, footsteps and voices, the open sounds of a public place. I guessed she was calling from a pay phone at the bottom of a stairwell.

"So, your mom told me you're an investigative reporter," she said.

"Did she?" And in that instant I wanted to tell Thea that my mother was wrong, that I'd been lying to her. *Nothing's going right,* I wanted to say. *Two days ago everything I worked for blew up in my face.*

I wanted to tell her about St. John and Ritger and their brand of mean-spirited journalism. I wanted to go back to the summer of 1985, when I could tell her my secrets, and start over from there. But a moment later, I felt foolish for having allowed such thoughts into my head.

"Tomorrow I start a long rotation at the hospital," she said. "I wanted to know if you'll have dinner with me tonight."

The invitation took me by surprise, so without thinking I said yes, sure, that would be fine.

"Eight o'clock at Arcobasso's?" she asked. "It's in Soulard."

"I know Arcobasso's." The restaurant was only a couple of blocks from my apartment. "It'll be good to see you."

It had been four years.

I made a mental note of it, hung up the phone, and rushed out the door, late for the funeral.

Crawley's Funeral Home was a converted rambler next to a Dunkin' Donuts near one of the older neighborhoods in suburban St. Charles. Its structure was made of smooth brick in various shades of tan and brown. A matching pair of windowless additions, covered in white siding, arched back from the main building, running parallel on either side. From behind, where I pulled around to park, the place looked like a giant magnet.

I cut the engine and waited for the Gremlin's shudders to subside. A silver hearse was parked out back, and a man in a gray pinstriped suit leaned against it smoking a cigarette. He looked at his watch, took a long drag from his cigarette, and with a smokeless exhale flicked the ashes to the ground, rolling the filter into a handkerchief. Straightening his fat-knotted tie, he walked in the back entrance under a green awning with the words RICHARD P. CRAWLEY AND SON, FUNERALS OF QUIET DIGNITY.

Despite my occupation, I had never been inside a funeral home. When my father was dying, we were living in Chicago, and I was sent away to Greencastle, Indiana, my mother's hometown, to stay with my aunt's family. Uncle Keith, my mother's brother-in-law, arrived the day my father went into the hospital, packed me a duffel bag of summer and fall clothes, and brought me down from the city on a rush-hour train. The one memory that sticks in my mind from that summer was that the neighbors had an above-ground pool and I panicked when they tried to teach me to swim. I stayed a month with my cousins, who were in high school then and didn't have much time for me, a five-year-old then. When I returned to Chicago, my father had died, and three weeks later I was shuttled back on the train, in a daze, this time to Columbia, Missouri, and to a new life in the college town where my parents had first met.

Why my mother had sent me away that summer was not an easy subject to talk about, so mostly we didn't. But it came up early one morning, my first year of high school, on what would have been my father's forty-fifth birthday. It was as though she suddenly felt compelled to say something, and I suppose she took a gamble that I'd now be mature enough to understand. She sat on the edge of my bed and, pressing out the wrinkles in the cover, explained that the doctors had told her he could live another three weeks or three months with this kind of cancer.

"I wasn't going to let you watch that," she said. "I wanted you to remember him the way he was: strong and tall and clear-eyed."

I told her I understood, which wasn't entirely true.

I had been to church funerals — for my uncle and my grandmother in Wichita, for the dean of the journalism school, for Mary Ellen of Mary Ellen's Beauty Shop, who did my mother's hair, and for a boy in my class who once put mashed potatoes in my milk and whose rope swing broke over rocks along the Gasconade.

In the sporadic car rides to Greencastle and Wichita to visit my family and up to Wisconsin where I went to camp one summer, I came to understand that the town is directly ahead when you see the graveyard and that the oldest, most beautiful house is always the funeral home.

It surprised me, then, since she had seemed like a woman of particular taste, that Alicia would have chosen this place to honor her husband — this house of mismatched parts at the edge of an outdated strip mall.

The funeral director, who had been smoking behind the building, greeted me at the front entrance. He had crust under his eyes, age spots along the sides of his face, a sore like dried preserves on his upper lip.

"Gunther or Whiting?" he asked, squinting from the brightness of the open door.

"Whiting," I said.

"Come with me." He took my elbow, leading me down a dark hallway. "Whiting is in the West Annex."

We stopped under a gold-veined mirror. He handed me a pen and pointed to an open guest book surrounded by peach gladioli.

"Please sign your name before entering the receiving room. The service will begin in fifteen minutes," he said, retreating.

For some reason, I hesitated about writing my own name, worried it might be traced back to me, so instead I signed my father's, "Charlie Hatch," near the bottom of the page.

When I opened the door and stepped inside the receiving room, I realized that the Dunkin' Donuts and the aluminum siding and the funeral director with the sore on his lip had all been there for good reason — to give this sanctuary at the end of the dark hallway the advantage of surprise.

Everywhere I looked there were white roses: white roses on the altar, a white rose on every chair, sprays of white roses in crystal vases, fans of white roses tied with purple ribbons on each of the velvet-draped tables.

I stood behind two middle-aged women who appeared to know each other. The one in front of me pulled some tissues from her purse and slipped them into her jacket, then turned around, handing me a program from the table beside her. Her friend, so large she obscured my view of the left side of the room, was speaking in a whisper to someone I couldn't see. I opened the program, glanced over it, and as another mourner came up behind me to take his place in line, I lifted my head — and there was Alicia.

She wore a navy crepe dress and a black cloche pulled low over her forehead, half of her face in shadow. Her lips were slightly parted, the flesh around her eyes soft with crying. She looked off toward the altar, in the center of which sat a mahogany cremation box.

The sight of her under the hat with her faraway expression in that bright, quiet room, which she had so artfully transformed, moved me to do the most curious thing: I kissed her hand.

I've never been a courtly person, have always found courtliness to be contrived, but I actually took her hand and pressed my lips to her fingers.

I have no idea what got into me, but there I was, at the funeral of a man I had never met, holding the hand of his wife, a woman I hardly knew, looking at her as if the world should step aside and leave us alone.

And she went straight along, as if kissing her hand were the most natural gesture for me to have made. She tilted her head and held my eyes for a moment. "I'm so glad you came." She sounded genuinely relieved.

"Of course," I said.

Standing next to her, the top of its head level with her elbow and baring its teeth, was the largest dog I had ever seen.

He had a rough, brindle coat, a long body, and a deep chest. His narrow face had wiry hairs that came together like extra fangs, and his small, high-set ears were drawn back against his neck.

"Gavin!" Alicia scolded, pointing a finger at the growling wolf-hound, who immediately sank to the floor.

She took my hand again. "He gets jealous," she whispered apologetically.

A cello was playing as Alicia introduced me to Joe Whiting, a tall bald man with a thin mustache, and Margaret, Arthur's sister, a rigid-looking woman with wire-rimmed glasses.

"This is the newspaper reporter Gordon Hatch," Alicia said. "He'll be writing the feature article for the St. Louis paper."

Joe Whiting nodded approvingly, making a strange sound in the back of his throat.

I said how sorry I was, how I had heard such wonderful things about his brother.

The sister, Margaret, shook my hand with surprising strength.

"A feature article? That's interesting." She folded her large-knuckled fingers in front of her, the expression on her face vaguely ironic. "I had no idea Arthur was feature material."

I looked down at my program, folding it in half. "Our feature stories tend to be community-oriented," I said.

She lifted a hand to her chin. A small black purse hung tidily from her elbow. "Community-oriented. Ah, I see."

She had an angular face and a sharp nose, a long sinewy neck, and she was taller than I by several inches. Her shoulder-length black hair was going gray and cut in severe bangs above her eyebrows. Her billowy black dress flared to the knees. Next to Alicia, she towered.

"What section of the paper are you with?" she asked, taking off her glasses.

"I work for Metro," I lied. "I'm on general assignment. I just go where they ask me to go."

"They?" She opened her purse and slid the glasses into a leather case.

"Assignment editors," I said.

"Oh." She smiled, but not in a friendly way, more to say, *Perhaps this can all be explained at a more appropriate time.*

I took a seat across the room next to the middle-aged women from the receiving line.

"He looks well," said the big one.

"Yes, he seems to be holding up," the other agreed.

"He's a remarkable specimen, even under duress."

I realized that they were talking about the dog.

"Do you think this means Arthur's wife will take over the society newsletter?" the large one asked.

"I can't imagine," said the other, lifting a Kleenex to cover her mouth. "She's a better-than-average groomer, but she has scant knowledge of the breed."

The service was sparsely attended. No more than twenty-five people had come. One of the bank managers at Portage Savings eulogized Arthur as a model of fairness and good citizenship and said that his performance during the bank robbery showed "a natural impulse for courage."

The minister, Reverend C. W. Johnson, gave a reading from Lamentations and said a few words about Arthur, speaking of him in such general terms that I assumed the two had never met. A cellist played "Fairest Lord Jesus," and a breeder from Mississippi Valley Irish Wolfhounds recalled the day nine years before when Arthur drove out to see a litter of puppies and walked away with majority ownership of his farm.

"He told me, flat out, he'd never even owned a breeding farm before," Clyde Hermann said, tugging at his shirt as though his tie were too tight. "But you know Arthur. He'd done all his research and he knew exactly what he wanted. I gave him my two best sires, and the rest is AKC history."

Margaret Whiting made a brief, somewhat chilling speech that seemed to end before it was meant to, as if her emotions would not allow her to say more. "As children Arthur and I were inseparable. I was born three years before him, but, like twins, we were connected at the core." Her voice trembled as she spoke. "To be happy in this world is to be understood," she said. "I understood my brother and my brother understood me." She looked down at her hands, clasped in front of her, then returned to her seat.

Alicia was sitting in the front row, several rows ahead of me, at an angle that made it difficult to see her face. The collar of her dress was pulled slightly down, exposing the back of her smooth neck, the notch at the top of her spine.

We all sang "O God Our Help in Ages Past." Toward the end of the service, during the moment of silence, I opened my program.

On the inside page was a poem I knew well. My mother had torn it from a book of romantic verse by Elizabeth Barrett Browning and taped it to the dining room wall when we moved into 102 La Grange:

> How do I love thee? Let me count the ways.
> I love thee to the depth and breadth and height
> My soul can reach, when feeling out of sight
> For the ends of Being and ideal Grace.
>   . . . I love thee with the breath,
> Smiles, tears, of all my life! — and, if God choose,
> I shall but love thee better after death.

I realized that for all the years that poem had hung on the dining room wall, I had never stopped to read it through, to consider it for what it was: the story of my mother's life.

The service over, Alicia exited through a side door carrying the small box with her husband's ashes. The wolfhound walked beside her, stride for stride, on tiptoe. Joe and Margaret Whiting followed, then the bank manager and the dog breeder and a woman in a tweed suit, then Reverend Johnson, who gestured for us all to rise and join them.

Alicia stood under the green awning with Joe Whiting, who was handing out directions to the Whispering Pines Country Club, where a reception would be held at six o'clock.

"I hope to see you there," she said solemnly.

"Of course I'll come."

And with that, the dinner plans I had made with Thea Pierson earlier in the day must have flown from my mind.

I couldn't leave work until the six-thirty meeting, so it was just after seven before I arrived at Whispering Pines, a modest country club with nine holes of golf, a swimming pool, and a rambling clubhouse, white brick with a green roof.

The reception was held in a dark room behind the ninth tee, where, through the sliding glass doors, we could see the last foursome of the day taking practice swings, polishing their three irons in the evening dusk.

A few guests stood around the buffet, a couple more perched uncomfortably on couches. Joe Whiting, a glass of Coke in his hand, was looking out at the golfers.

"How are you?" I asked.

"Me?" He turned around, pulling his head back, giving me a confused look.

He was maybe six foot four, with a long chin, high cheekbones, and the same large Adam's apple as his brother. He wore glasses now, squarish, thick-rimmed bifocals with a strong prescription, too big for his face. He had a smooth, shiny head, gray hairs around his temples; his pencil mustache was jet black.

"What a beautiful service," I said.

He seemed to have no recollection of meeting me. "Oh, yes. Yes,

that's right. A beautiful service. It provided a service for all of us."
He smiled broadly, holding his drink with two hands, bowing as he
spoke. "For those of us in the service industry, it was a particularly
good service. It was quite serviceable." He laughed.

"I see," I said, quickly scanning the room for Alicia or Margaret
or anyone to help explain what I hadn't realized about Joe.

"Is Alicia here?" I asked.

"I like Alicia. She has pretty hair, and she gives me treats." He
wrinkled his nose. "They're treats for dogs. You can't eat these
kinds of treats. They're disgusting to eat."

Joe reached into his pocket and pulled out a handful of dog
snacks, and I saw for the first time that he was dressed in work
clothes: heavy boots and a pair of navy Dickies and a gray shirt
with mud streaked on it. Someone must have lent him the blazer
he was wearing.

"You're in the service industry?" I offered, indulging him because his outfit and his mustache, so conspicuously dyed, and his
labored enthusiasm made me sad.

"I'm in the industrious industry," he said. "I'm very industrious.
You can ask anyone."

Joe carried on in this way, and I learned that he worked for
Clyde, the breeder who had spoken at the funeral, on a farm up
near Winfield. He gave me all the names of Arthur's dogs and the
prizes they'd won, speaking in the most cheerful manner, pausing
only to push his glasses up his nose or take a two-handed sip of his
drink, and I began to wonder if a person like Joe would be capable
of feeling sadness.

"Arthur worked in a bank. He has my arrowhead on his desk,"
he said at one point, speaking of Arthur in both the past and present tense, giving no indication that he understood the loss.

Joe spotted Alicia first. She was huddled in a far corner of the
room speaking with the woman in the tweed suit from the morning. The wolfhound lay at her feet with a despondent look.

"Margaret's at the hotel, because she hates Alicia." He nudged me. "She said she was going to the service and that's that. 'That's that,' she said. Excuse me, I need to go to the bathroom.'"

Before he left, I asked him where Margaret was staying and gave him my phone number in case he ever wanted to call, realizing as I was writing it down that this was probably a mistake.

On the way out I noticed that Alicia and the dog were now engaged in what appeared to be a serious conversation. She was looking down at the floor, scratching the dog's face in long, slow strokes from the tip of his nose to the back of his head. His eyes blinked and closed, a contented smile set on his grizzled face.

I started toward them, then hesitated, suddenly tense, deciding we could catch up later. And after a couple of mini ham sandwiches and some oversweet punch, I briefly complimented Reverend Johnson on the service and left Whispering Pines.

Out on the highway, the road was empty, the slow lane all mine, and I rolled the windows down to take in some of the cool October air.

Somehow, it had been an exhilarating day. I didn't know what it meant to fall in love, couldn't remember how it had felt with Thea, except that at the time it was safer than "falling." I'd always been a cautious person, alert to the dangers of the world. But falling was the sense I had of things now.

I couldn't get Alicia out of my mind — in her hat at the funeral, in her burgundy dress, her small hand reaching out, fast forward across my line of vision. Her voice kept turning over in my head. I thought of Czechoslovakia, of where I'd go for lunch tomorrow, of who I'd be five years from now, every possibility colored by thoughts of Alicia, as if we had made an arrangement together, as if she were somehow mine to consider and not the bereaved widow of Arthur Whiting. I knew it was crazy, but there she was, playing on me.

Back home, I threw my jacket on the couch and checked the answering machine. The message light read 2.

I listened to the long squeal of the machine rewinding, wondering why Alicia would have left two messages and figured the first one had been cut off. I worried she might be upset that I didn't talk to her at the reception.

"This is your mother," the machine said, and I knew it meant trouble. "Thea just called from a restaurant down the street from you. She's been waiting forty-five minutes and I've told her to leave —"

I cut it off there, skipping ahead to the second message.

The voice was Thea's.

I pressed the rewind button — I couldn't stand to listen — and fell back in my bed.

8

ON WEDNESDAY MORNING, I printed out the seventy-nine advancers, single-spaced, reduced to a small point size, in the order I had written them. I planned to save them as a reminder of my potential.

On my chair sat a piece of pink notepaper, folded in half and stapled, with "Gordon Hatch, Obituary Desk" written in a leaning cursive.

> Dear Gordon Hatch,
>   I was appalled by the way you were treated yesterday. From my observations, you are a hard-working young man who does his part and does it quietly. Nobody deserves to be pilloried like that, least of all someone whose only offense was making a positive change. If you care for an audience or if you need anything, I am at your service.
>
>   Regards,
>   Jessie Tennant

I could see that Jessie Tennant's computer was signed off, her desk cleared; a bottle of Windex stood at the end of a neat row of reference books. Photographs of Sarah Vaughan and Rosa Parks and a postcard print of a toppled yellow rocking chair were pressed next to a calendar under the heavy glass on her desk.

I never respond well to acts of kindness. I wish I could look a person in the eye in a way that says, *What a decent gesture — one day I'll do the same for you or for someone else with you in mind,* but invariably I'm embarrassed by the attention and go out of my way to avoid an encounter. Still, I was comforted to know that I had an in-house supporter.

After starting and scrapping several longer messages, I managed to write back, through interoffice mail, "Dear Jessie Tennant, Thank you very much for your nice note. With gratitude, Gordon Hatch."

I organized my advancers and slipped them into an envelope along with Jessie Tennant's note. I sealed the envelope, rotating it, feeling its impressive weight in my hands, and in black felt marker wrote,

ADVANCERS
September 13, 1988–October 5, 1989
R. Nixon through J. DiMaggio

and tucked the envelope in the pocket of my briefcase.

I had forgotten about the photo of Arthur Whiting that Alicia had left for me at the security desk that first night she called. I took another look at it now — his small eyes, the sharp angles of his face. He did resemble his sister, Margaret, though the similarity had less to do with features than with a common edge, an intensity they seemed to share. The first time I had seen his photograph, he had reminded me of those daguerreotypes of Old West home-steaders. Tall, drawn, remote, even a bit lost. But now I saw a fervor in his eyes that I hadn't recognized before.

I slipped the photograph back into the envelope, and as I did so, I could feel something else at the bottom of the package. I reached in to pull out a folded piece of paper. I assumed that it would be a pleasant note from Alicia, thanking me for placing her husband's obit, but as I opened it I saw a grid — one of Arthur's weekly schedules.

Attached to the schedule was a yellow Post-it note. "Copy and send to Margaret." Someone, I assumed Alicia, had written it in a hasty print. Typed along the top of the spreadsheet was "Schedule for the Week of September 30 to October 6, 1989." It was partially filled out, through Wednesday, October 2. I got the chills thinking of Arthur at his computer working on this document not knowing that he would die the next day. I wondered if his own hand had touched this same piece of paper.

Alicia had described these schedules well. Every half hour was accounted for. Monday night they had watched a video, *On the Waterfront*. Under the title of the film, Arthur had written, "Elia Kazan, director/ Marlon Brando, male lead/ Eva Marie Saint, female lead." He had gone to bed at 11:30 after reading *Discovery* magazine for half an hour. The next day at 7:30 A.M. he had returned the video before going to work. For lunch he had chili, for dinner that night pasta primavera, which he had cooked. Tuesday and Wednesday evenings he had "worked on the newsletter," but was no more specific than that. Peppered throughout the grid were trips to the park with the dog, daily one-hour sessions on a stationary bike followed by the *NBC Nightly News*, and long blocks, thoroughly notated, describing the work that he did at the bank — "Kinney IRA," "Walker account," "Promissory notes from NDSL."

I added Arthur's grid to the other envelope along with my advancers and the note from Jessie Tennant, then went about my morning chores — reading the obits from Kansas City and the suburban weeklies, looking over the story budget, sifting through the mail, checking the fax machine and the AP wires, losing myself in the day's repetitions.

When I returned from lunch, there was a message on my desk from Thea, left by one of the switchboard operators.

"The flowers are beautiful. They just arrived. Thank you. Apology accepted."

I immediately called my mother at the journalism school.

"You're unbelievable," I said.

"What?"

"You're really beyond help." I hunched over the desk so I wouldn't be heard.

"What did you send her?" I asked. "A dozen red roses? A note saying I'm sorry and I'll always love you? I wonder if you're ever going to quit."

"Look, Gordie, don't give me that attitude."

"What did you tell her?" I asked. "Where did you say I was?"

"I'm the one who should be angry," she said. "Don't turn this on me."

"I'm not turning it on you, but this is none of your business. She called me! It was our dinner date! I'm the one who needs to deal with this."

"Listen, you made it my business by not showing up."

My mother's voice had an annoyingly even pitch when we fought. The more excited I became, the calmer her voice. She spoke her words slowly, as if my poor comprehension required such care.

"She called me because she was concerned about you," she said.

"What about you? Why weren't you concerned about me?" I shot back, recognizing my mistake.

"I knew you were home by ten because I called you twice," she said. "Your machine sounds different when the messages have been erased. Why weren't you picking up the phone, Gordie?"

I had no answer.

"So have you called her?" Her tone was nagging again.

"I plan to call her, Mother. I've been incredibly busy."

"What happened?"

"I forgot, okay? It slipped my mind. I talked to her in the morning. Everything was all set. Around midday I had to go to St. Charles for an investigative piece I'm working on. I had an interview with a witness and totally lost track of time."

"What's the story?" she asked.

"I can't tell you right now. I'm at work."

"I just wish you had called her when you got my message."

Apparently, my mother had woken Thea at one in the morning to say that I was too ashamed to call but had just returned to the apartment from a surveillance mission. She said I had been tailing a certain high-level official in the city government who, I had reason to believe, was involved in money laundering, that I'd followed him in the car from his office to a warehouse on the other side of the river, watched him enter the place through a rusted-out door, and couldn't help myself from going in behind him.

She said I had moved in his shadow along the corrugated walls of the warehouse, hiding behind some boxes next to an office with no door. A host of suspicious types emerged from the office, fanning out around the warehouse to stand guard. The meeting lasted from midday until well into the night and there was nothing I could do; I was stuck with no way out. The whole time I sat crouched behind those boxes, my life in danger, unable to make a sound, I had one eye on my watch thinking, "What will I ever tell Thea?"

"I hated to lie, Gordie," my mother said. "But I had to tell her something."

"Well, it was very imaginative," I said.

Back at my apartment that night, I wanted to call Thea to apologize, but my mother had made that impossible. I should have been angry with her for meddling in my affairs as she always did, but this time I could only blame myself.

My alarm clock was at exactly 9:00 when I sat up from the living room couch. I waited for the red numbers to read 9:01, then swung my legs around and got up to make myself dinner. Most nights when I made dinner for myself, my repertoire generally limited to prepackaged meals for one — Swedish meatballs, pepper steak, macaroni and cheese — I turned on my scanner and listened to the police channels with the soft hum of the microwave in the background.

Not many obit writers have a need for a scanner, but toward the end of summer I had become obsessed with its macabre details, tuning in every night from dinner until bedtime. It was vicarious adventure, but thrilling all the same.

When the homicide unit was called, I would feel a rush, imagine the scene — a police officer cordoning off the entrance to a run-down housing complex. "What's the victim's name?" I'd ask, and coolly display my *Independent* ID.

The phone rang as I was pulling my Swedish meatballs out of the microwave.

"What were you going to tell me this afternoon?" my mother asked.

"About what?" I cut open one of the packages, sliding the noodles onto a plate.

"About this story you're working on," she said.

"It's nothing, Mother. Just a little human interest story. No big deal."

"That's not what you told me this afternoon," she said. "You implied you were on to something important."

I cut open the meatballs, poured them over the noodles, distributed the gravy evenly with a fork.

"Can't we talk about this when I'm further along with the investigation?" I said, filling a glass with milk. "It should be at least another couple of weeks. I'd rather we talk about it later."

But she wouldn't let it alone. I sat on a stool at the kitchen counter, and as I held the receiver away from my mouth and quietly chewed, she reminded me of how much more my father had achieved by this point in his career.

"I realize it was a different time then," she said. "Newspapers have gotten very competitive, but it only took him eight months before his byline was everywhere."

I slid my plate aside.

"I know you have to pay your dues," she was saying. "But your father had a great instinct, and that's what put him above —"

I cut her off. "To be honest, I'm trying to finish dinner here, so I didn't want to go too deeply into it, but since you're so anxious, I may as well tell you that this story I'm working on *is* beginning to look like a breakthrough."

I told her that I'd been snooping around at City Hall and had found a source who was talking about some unaccounted-for campaign funds. "Let's just say that the mayor's brother has suddenly found himself rich," I said.

My lie wasn't even original; the story came directly from a piece I'd seen in the *Tennessean.* The mayor of Nashville had set up a fund for his contractor brother, and millions of campaign dollars had ended up in a golfing development for country-and-western stars.

"Whatever you do, don't tell anyone in the J-school," I said. "This has to stay quiet while I get more details."

And that wasn't all. I told her that my name kept coming up for a beat job, that I'd been making inroads with police administration, that I was keeping sharp with hard news by showing up at crime scenes and assisting the cop reporters. "I look at Obits as a day job," I said.

I wasn't sure what had gotten into me, and already I was feeling the metallic queasiness of guilt. First Thea and now the lies I had to tell. My mother used to know everything — we kept no secrets between us — but now with my career under way, separated by a hundred miles, I no longer needed her reminders.

When we hung up, I waited for something to happen on the scanner's reports. Anything. That night I had to go to a crime scene.

The call came around eleven o'clock: two cars needed at the river-bank north of downtown. One wounded for sure. I grabbed my ID on my way out of the apartment to the Gremlin, not bothering to wait for the next wave of information.

I expected to find the victim along one of the cobbled lanes of Laclede's Landing, the bar and club district just north of the Gateway Arch. He'd be sitting up against one of the old-fashioned streetlamps holding his wounded arm and answering questions. Three policemen would have a suspect pinned against a nearby wall. The guy would be slurring something like, "He had it coming." And that would be that. My first crime scene.

But the map didn't lead me to Laclede's Landing. It took me farther north, up Memorial Drive past the Adams Mark and the bars on Wharf Street, up the river along the eastern edges of The Ville, where Tina Turner had sung in the choir and Chuck Berry learned to duckwalk, where Annie Malone made her first million. It took me far from the city, down a dark street that dead-ended near the riverbank. I pulled the Gremlin up to the levee and turned off my headlights. Forty yards downriver, lit by a high three-quarter moon, stood a half-dozen figures circling a white bundle. From the car, it looked like a nativity scene.

I got out, quietly shut the door, and took a few cautious steps forward. A police cruiser had pulled up ahead of me, cutting his lights, and an officer jumped out to join the huddle. Moving closer, I noticed that all of the figures were police officers. They stood around as if waiting for something, talking casually among themselves, laughing, shifting their heaviness from foot to foot.

Off to the right, hidden by the long shadow of the McKinley Bridge, were three more figures, somber and removed, looking on in silence. I approached the first one, a big-bellied guy, glowering in his Army jacket and Budweiser cap. He had a permanent lean to the left.

"I'm with the *Independent*," I said. "Can you tell me what happened here?"

"You're what?" he spat.

"I'm a reporter," I said, feeling my chest tighten. "I want to know what happened."

His upper lip was curled over broken teeth.

"I'm with the *Independent*," I repeated, taking a step backward, as if doing so would rewind and start the scene again, this time with me in charge, the way I had always imagined it.

One of the men standing behind him stepped around and introduced himself. "Dr. Osborn." He held out his hand and smiled. "We've got a shooting victim. No suspects," he said. "The sheet's mine. I always keep a few in the trunk."

"What branch of law enforcement are you with?" I asked.

He shrugged. "No branch. But I come when they call."

He was thickset and jowly and looked out of place in his yellow sweater and tartan pants. A pair of half-spectacles hung from his neck on a helical chain.

"So, what did the victim look like?" I asked, thinking I'd need a physical description for my write-up.

"Black male, late teens, same as always," he said, lowering his chin, holding my stare under his pale brow. "They shot him execution style, probably knocked him off his bicycle first. It's over there." He pointed up the levee beyond the white bundle where the bicycle lay on its side.

It occurred to me that this was all my mother's fault, that she had driven me to coming here. How would she feel, I wondered, if she could see me alone in this place, with these treacherous people, the police joking about a dead body at their feet?

"Who shot him?" I asked. A bloodstain in the shape of a kidney was spreading near the top of the white bundle.

"Like I said, no suspects." Dr. Osborn shrugged.

The third figure stepped up, mousy and squint-eyed. He said he had taken some pictures. "You're with the newspaper, right?" His voice was staccato. "You probably want what I got."

I looked down at his crazy, matted hair, his rough face, as he lifted the camera off his neck.

"See, I took pictures. You wanna see my work? I've got *all* kinds of pretty pictures. Here, look at this!" He shook his camera. "You want front page? I've got front page right here!"

"Lucas is a photographer," Dr. Osborn said as the mousy man bent down, rifling through a gym bag.

"Ah!" Lucas lofted a photo album in the air, then brought it over and shoved it at me.

He pulled a flashlight from his back pocket and handed it to me. "My portfolio," he said, and took a little bow. "If you want names, I've got names for each one. Let me get my book."

As he returned to the gym bag I brought the flashlight up to the smudged pages of his photo album. They were all shooting victims. Some dead, some alive, some covered with a sheet. Some were taken from a distance, some right up close.

I shut the book, feeling lightheaded, and handed it over as he returned.

"What do you want?" he said. "What do you need to know?"

Before I could respond, there was a hand on my shoulder. "Hatch! What the hell are *you* doing here?"

I sprang back and turned the flashlight on the *Independent*'s police reporter, Marshall Holman.

"Didn't know you lived in The Ville." He laughed.

I lowered the flashlight, handing it back to Lucas.

"These dudes friends of yours?" Holman asked.

He took my arm and led me closer to the huddle of police officers, who paid no attention to us. We stopped by one of the squad cars. "You know who those guys are, don't you?" He nodded back at Dr. Osborn and friends.

"No."

"They're ghouls. That's all they are. Sick mugs who get off on crime scenes."

I looked over my shoulder. The one in the Budweiser hat was flipping through the photo album.

"They sit around their apartments listening to the scanner,"

Holman went on. "When they hear 'homicide,' they crank up their jalopies and race to get to the crime scene first. Sometimes they even beat the police. Then it's Vincent Price Theater until the coroner comes."

One of the police officers had gone over to look at the bicycle. I was beginning to feel nauseated.

"Three ghouls is par for the course." Holman pulled a cellular phone from his windbreaker. "I've seen as many as eight at one time. The big one in the pants drives a Crown Victoria. He's got everything in there: scanner, a little TV, telephone. He goes to pretty much all of them."

He punched some buttons on his cellular. Up close, in the moonlight, he looked much larger than I had remembered him from the newsroom, with a powerful neck that tensed when he spoke and a three-day beard that glistened.

"This damn thing better work."

"Trouble?" I asked.

"It's the battery."

I shrugged, thinking of other ways to change the subject.

"So what *are* you doing here?" Holman asked.

I looked up at the bridge, across the river to Illinois, and let the silence hang in the air for a moment. "A tipster called me," I said.

"What do you mean, a tipster?" He put the phone to his ear.

"It's confidential," I said. "Someone I've been working with. I'd love to tell you about it, but I can't."

Holman put his hand up as the night editor's voice came over the receiver. "One second." He held the phone away from his mouth.

I began to move back toward the Gremlin.

"See you in the newsroom." I waved. He held up a finger to say *hold on,* but I was already walking briskly away.

Back on the road to St. Louis, my fuel tank was nearly empty. I hadn't counted on going anywhere that night and had forgotten that I'd let it get so low. Rolling down the deserted streets of The

Ville, I cursed my mother and the police and the city for not having more streetlights out here. I cursed the people hidden away in their darkened houses, the buildings and storefronts all locked and barred now, and the Gremlin for being an old car without a fuel light to assure me that I'd make it a few more miles.

"Come on," I coaxed, begging for a gas station to rise out of the darkness.

I flew through the blinking yellow lights at the intersections. Shredded tires and hubcaps lay strewn along the divider. Plastic grocery bags caught the wind and danced in the air like ghosts. Peeling billboards lined the roads — YOUR ADVERTISEMENT HERE and WORRY NO MORE ABOUT BAD CREDIT.

This would be life for the last person on earth.

I leaned over the wheel to keep my eyes off the sunken fuel gauge and thought about the ghouls and Holman and the police officers laughing over the stained white bundle. I pictured the photo album, its stilled images of death, heard the echo of Dr. Osborn casually describing how this boy was shot off his bicycle.

In the distance, where the streets began to widen, where The Ville gave way to the northern edge of the St. Louis commercial district, I saw the red, white, and black of a Texaco station sign. Coasting in neutral down a small hill, the red Texaco star large against the night sky, I pulled the Gremlin under the bright lights of the service island, promising myself I'd never go to another crime scene.

9

THE NEXT DAY the temperature dropped into the forties. That
night we had our first hard frost, and by the weekend the leaves
had begun to turn. It was only mid-October, but already you could
see the alertness in people that comes with the first real chill in the
air, that sense of purpose anticipating change.

Where I grew up in Columbia, fall had been characterized by
football Saturdays and the hapless Missouri Tigers, who would
draw sellout crowds of middle-aged diehards in gold and black jer-
seys. They would park on our street, six blocks from the stadium,
and stumble back four hours later from yet another trouncing,
with empty souvenir cups in their hands. The smell of fall for me
had been Budweiser and cheap mustard and tailgate bratwurst
that floated downwind from the stadium into our open garage. In
Columbia, fall lasted a full twelve weeks, six home games and six
away, ending on the final Saturday in November, with a fight for
last place with the Kansas State Wildcats.

But in St. Louis, the pro football team had moved to Phoenix a
year ago and the season seemed cloudy and short. Without the
smell of football in the air, fall was a four-week bridge between
summer and winter, a shame for a city whose buildings seemed
made with autumn's colors in mind. Like most of the old Mississippi River trading towns, St. Louis was built largely of brick —

brown-red brick for the warehouses near the river, orange brick for the old downtown office buildings, yellow brick for the neighborhood row houses — colors to match the leaves falling off maples and oaks, sweetgums and birches that grew tall and exuberant along the city's avenues. Even the siding on the suburban ranch houses was made to look like some shade of brick.

One such house belonged to Alicia Whiting.

In the days following my visit to the crime scene, having already been humiliated once, I had begun to consider the possibility that I might actually fail at becoming a reporter. Increasingly, my mind was turning toward Alicia.

I kept going back to her first phone call, when she had convinced me of her husband's importance. She had been so certain, deluded by her own grief into thinking Arthur was extraordinary, that of course I had believed her. When it turned out that Arthur was just another man who worked in a bank, I didn't feel deceived. I had a predisposed sympathy for young widows, after all, since I had grown up with one.

I felt a natural protectiveness for Alicia almost right away. She had an unexpected quality, an odd combination of formality and freedom, cardigans and chiming bangles, white flowers and ticky-tack, grand observations followed by self-mockery. And, for some reason, those contradictions set me at ease, made me do things I wouldn't ordinarily do. Vulnerability and overriding grief were not qualities I usually found myself drawn to. But Alicia seemed to have something. Who knew? Maybe even a story.

On Saturday, a week after her first phone call, three days after meeting the ghouls, I looked up her number in the St. Charles White Pages: 324-9679. I copied it into my address book and practiced dialing it with the receiver still in the cradle. The more times I dialed, the more familiar her number became, my fingers memorizing the zigzag path across the phone pad.

What were the odds, I wondered, of getting her answering machine? I wanted to get her answering machine — I had to know whose voice was on the outgoing message, Alicia's or Arthur's? I figured if it was her voice, she'd be ready to hear from me.

Alicia had said in our first conversation that lately she never left the house. Still, if she was there all day, I wondered if she even answered the phone. At a time like this, wouldn't she screen her calls? I could listen and hang up. If she answered, I could hang up too, divining her emotional state from the tone of her voice.

But just as soon as I summoned the courage to call, I worried that a new widow would be extra-sensitive to a hang-up. She might have the call traced. The police could show up at my apartment, or worse, they'd find me at the obituary desk.

Instead, at the library I discovered a detailed map of St. Charles County. The city of St. Charles sits ten miles north of St. Louis, just below the confluence of the Missouri and Mississippi rivers. The Whitings lived on Dalecarlia Drive, which lay near the middle of St. Charles, off Kingshighway, a few blocks beyond the old section along the Missouri known as Frenchtown. I made a copy of the map and for three days carried it around in my briefcase.

I suppose I had in mind that something might happen between Alicia and me. I cleaned my apartment, paid my bills early, bought wine and candles and a poster for my bedroom from the movie *Top Hat* — Fred Astaire, in tux and tails, dancing across a marble floor; Ginger Rogers, in an ankle-length dress, twirling out of his arms.

At work, I made myself busy, meeting deadlines, acting deferential toward Ritger and St. John. And I sent Marshall Holman a missive through in-house mail:

Dear Marshall,
  You must have been surprised to see me at that crime scene the other night, so I thought I'd explain myself. It had nothing to do with what happened recently in the conference room. St. John and I had a little misunderstanding, and I'm sorry that the whole event took place.
  I said before that a tipster had called me. I'd been at the office

doing research when the city desk phone started ringing incessantly. I'm not sure where your editor was at the time — maybe getting coffee — but the tip, which I now realize was bogus, required a reporter at the scene immediately. I didn't know how to reach you, so I went myself. You must get these false alarms all the time.

Just an overexcited obituary writer,
Gordon Hatch

In the nights after my trip to The Ville, I'd kept to my old routine, falling asleep to the crackle of the police radio, still imagining myself at the scene. But I had not gone out again. A week later, I dreamt that I was a figure from one of the pictures in Lucas's photo album. An eight-by-ten shot that filled the page. The ghouls were laughing at me, at my lifeless face and body curled up on a black tile floor. I sat up in bed and turned on the light. I knew then that I would drive to Alicia's the next day.

The city was under a sheet of gray when I left work at lunchtime the next afternoon, Thursday, October 17. The temperature had dropped several degrees, and by the time I crossed the bridge into St. Charles it was raining steadily. I was glad for the cover that the rain provided and relieved that I had, in the end, decided to rent a cellular phone, since I knew they were difficult to trace.

I pictured Alicia lying in her bedroom listening to the patter of rain on her roof. The rain would feel symbolic, almost personal, as if it were coming down only for her. She wouldn't have bothered to close any windows, letting the elements into her room.

As I crossed Kingshighway and turned onto Dalecarlia Drive, my heartbeat quickened. Number 436 Dalecarlia stood right there on the corner, surprisingly close. I drove to the end of the block, made a U-turn, pulled the Gremlin under a large orange-leafed maple half a block down from her house.

I had brought a newspaper to hide behind, thinking of movie stakeouts. But with the rain coming down hard now, my face through the windshield well obscured, the newspaper seemed hardly necessary.

Her house was a split-level, with a bay window and faux brick siding a shade of burnt yellow. An ordinary house, really, nearly identical to the one next door. The lawn had recently been cut. A high fence, barely weathered, surrounded the yard.

In the driveway sat a blue Delta 88.

I cut my lights, left the motor running. For a moment I was unable to move. She was home. She had to be.

The rain fell between us. Even so, I felt exposed. If she looked out onto the street at this moment, the way unhappy people are supposed to look out windows on rainy days, she would certainly see me. The light above her front door was on. The morning paper still lay on her doorstep.

I turned on the cellular phone and nervously dialed her number, my thumb on the red button ready to cut off the call. It rang once, then again, then I realized — Alicia had seen my car before; she'd know it was me out here. I had parked the Gremlin in back of the funeral home where Alicia had stood under the green awning passing out directions. I had walked down the steps and climbed into my car. Surely she had watched me.

I could almost see her sitting at her bedroom window now, leaning out, squinting into the rain. I pressed the hang-up button, let down the hand brake, and drove slowly away.

That Sunday, I was relieved to be returning home to Columbia to see my mother. I had promised her a visit, and since I had nothing to do on my day off anyway but worry over my future and daydream about Alicia, I was happy for a change of scenery. Not that I was looking forward to being around my mother, who lately had been driving me crazy with her career harassment and her talk of Thea, but I knew I needed to leave St. Louis, if only for a day, to gain some perspective on what had been a whirlwind couple of weeks.

After an early start, I arrived at 102 La Grange before she was expecting me. From the living room came a loud wave of *The Pirates of Penzance:* "I am a Pirate King!" the stereo blared. "And it tis, it tis a glorious thing to be a Pirate King!" I went into the living room and turned the volume down.

"You're early," my mother said, emerging from the back hallway, the Sunday crossword in hand.

"The boarders must love that stuff." I flipped through the *Independent* that was sitting on the dinette and picked out the metro section.

"What stuff?" she asked.

"Gilbert and Sullivan."

"It's good for them," she said.

"At ten in the morning?" I sat on the living room couch and opened the paper to the obits. "They're graduate students. I assure you they're asleep."

"What kind of a greeting is this?"

"Sorry, Mother. One can only take so much 'taran-tara!' at this hour."

She sighed. "People don't appreciate language anymore. Plays on words," she said, turning the stereo off. "I sometimes wonder if the end of rhyme didn't go hand in hand with the end of happiness." She sat down next to me on the couch, throwing aside her mostly finished crossword puzzle, and gave me a quick hug.

"Cheer up." She smiled and then started singing half seriously: "Ah, leave me not to pine/ Alone and desolate;/ No fate seemed fair as mine,/ No happiness so great!"

"And what are you so happy about?" Music always cheered her up, but she seemed in particularly good spirits.

"Oh, nothing," she said. "I've been reading some old letters. Have you had breakfast? I had in mind a visit to Country Carl's."

Country Carl's was a diner on the other side of the university that I hadn't visited since college. There was a waitress named

Alma with a pile of red hair who called me "sugar" and my mother "darlin'." The cook was leaner than Jack Sprat, a poor endorsement for the food he was slapping together. Faded posters of meal platters, like the cole slaw, fries, and cheese surprise — a Velveeta-impregnated hamburger — plastered the walls. Country Carl's had such authentic atmosphere it seemed almost inauthentic.

My mother drank a cup of coffee while I gorged myself on a big plate of biscuits and gravy. I hadn't realized how long it had been since I'd had a genuine, mid-Missouri, cardiac-inducing breakfast.

"Disgusting, I know," I said.

"You're not eating well, are you? You look skinny."

"This won't exactly keep me skinny."

"The same thing happened to your father in Dallas. When he left Kansas he looked wonderful, but by March when I went out to join him in Texas, I swear he'd lost twenty pounds."

Alma brought the check, and I offered to pay the bill, but my mother wouldn't allow it. "So tell me about Thea," she said, calculating fifteen percent of the $6.50 total on the back of the check, an annoying and stingy habit she had.

"What's to tell? I still haven't seen her."

"But you will see her, won't you? She's moved to St. Louis to be near you, you realize."

I rolled my eyes. "St. Louis University has a very good hospital. It's cheap and close to home," I said. "I don't need the guilt trip, Mother. You know she didn't move there for me."

"But you've told me yourself that there's only one perfect person for everyone, Gordie." She slipped her pen into her purse. "Don't you still believe that?"

"I don't know."

"Of course you do. Your father was the one perfect person for me. I never had a doubt about that." She looked at me steadily. "Have you ever thought that Thea believes *you* are that one person?"

I slid out of the booth and put my jacket on. "I guess you never know," I said.

After breakfast, she dropped me off at the house, saying she needed to do a few things at the office and would be back shortly. I watched her drive off wondering why she was going to work when we had planned to spend the day together.

As it turned out, her leaving was completely in character. My mother loved nothing more than a dramatic presentation, and now I saw sitting on my bedroom desk a box marked "Charlie — Navy, 1959–1962." It was overflowing with yellowed notes and letters, correspondence I had never known existed. I couldn't help feeling like a voyeur, but it was clear that my mother had wanted to share them, to urge me in her odd way toward Thea, and to acknowledge that she thought my life was about to take off.

My parents had first met in 1958 in Columbia, where my father was finishing his degree in history. He hadn't known much about the journalism school until his final year, when he took a class in journalistic ethics that first sparked his interest in reporting. My mother, an actress and dancer at Stephens, a small liberal arts college in town, was three years younger than he.

I didn't know the particulars of their courtship. I had always considered it sacred ground, not for me to ask about, and my mother's stories dealt less with details than with the broader picture of their ideal romance. Still, I had always imagined that they met at my father's favorite bar, the Heidelberg, since closed down. The bar had been a block from the Stephens College Theater, and my mother had told me that she used to go there for cast parties after a show. I had always assumed that my father had been instantly smitten, had probably glimpsed her across the bar still playing the role of Maggie the Cat. And my mother, in turn, would have been drawn to this tall, clean-cut soon-to-be-graduate who could transform a room with a phrase. Theirs was an uncommon union, and when my father left for the Navy, my mother staying behind to finish her degree, their devotion to each other solidified all the more.

My father's telegrams and postcards were short and considered, nothing wasted, as though he had taken great care with the sentences. He wrote in a meticulous print, and I was pleased by the balance of his words, their measured emotion: "There's nothing more sad than the silence of this place without you," he wrote from New London. "I can't wait for the end of this silence and the beginning of our life together." They were full of private references that weren't difficult to decipher: "Sorry I'm so camera shy when you're so beautiful," he wrote on one note that must have accompanied a photograph. "Twelve days, seven hours, thirty-five minutes away," he signed off on another, dated May 1959, just before their wedding. "Now I know why they call it the blue, blue sea," he had sent, by Western Union telegram, from the South Pacific.

I was searching for his long dispatches about Navy life, as a kind of warm-up to his eventual work as a journalist. They would read like a special report in serial — a peacetime look at the naval apparatus, full of observations and history and keen insights — but none of those letters was here. For the most part, when he wasn't telling my mother how much he missed her, he was describing his mates or generally lamenting the tedium of his daily life.

My mother, on the other hand, had written long, rambling letters in loopy handwriting, full of florid passages, that I could only glance at before feeling embarrassed and moving on to the next. "I am thinking now of how, when you drive, you rest one hand at the top of the steering wheel and every so often lift it to glance at one of those gauges. What do they call them? Speedometer? Odometer? RPM? Always keeping watch."

Often, she would stop in the middle of a long reverie and step back to note how silly in love she was: "You must forgive my carrying on. What would the other fellows think of you if they were to catch a glimpse of this wonderful mush you get in the mail?

"The mush is everywhere and I surrender to it. I see it before me and I must plunge in. And it's all your fault, darling. You're the one who turns me to this. I try to put my feelings into words, to say how much I miss you, how my entire life begins in May 1962, when we'll be together forever, but at the end of my words there are only more words. Have I told you this before?"

In the summer of 1961, my father was posted at a base in the Marshall Islands. He loved the New York Yankees, having come of age in the era of DiMaggio, and he couldn't stand that he was out of the States during Maris and Mantle's chase of Babe Ruth's home run record. My mother, who admitted she didn't like baseball, would nevertheless listen to Yankee games on the radio and report back long descriptions in order to keep my father up-to-date. "Maris's 53rd was on a low outside pitch in the seventh inning. The count was two balls and two strikes," she wrote in one of the letters. "It was a line drive that cleared the left field wall by ten feet, giving the Yankees a 4–2 lead."

Interspersed with her game summaries, she imagined herself joining my father in the South Pacific. She wrote of them walking the beaches of Fiji, sailing a sloop over an archipelago, setting up camp on empty lagoons. In later letters, when he had returned to the States and she was in her last year of college, she fantasized about crossing the country on a motorcycle and riding down the coast with him to Florida. I couldn't help smiling at the image of my mother on a motorcycle, or even of my mother in love. She had always simply been my mother. It was strange to imagine her as anything else.

She never dated after my father died. At least not so far as I knew. She had suitors, but only the most self-abasing kind, men who sought out rejection. I remember meeting one of them, a furry little geology professor named Alvin Bosky, who had been begging her for months to have dinner with him. We were at a cocktail party after the Missouri Awards, the biggest event of the year at the journalism school, and I'll never forget the look she gave him when he approached her with two glasses of wine. It was a look that went beyond scolding, something a third-grade teacher might spend a lifetime getting right. A will-you-ever-learn look that settled into one much harsher: "you're miles below me." I had rarely seen her icy side and wondered if my being there hadn't encouraged her to drop the temperature a few dozen degrees. "We're just leaving," she had said, and grabbed my hand and walked away.

It's difficult to say, of course, but my guess is she chose not to remarry less because of me than for the fact that my father had been everything to her and no man could live up to that standard.

The door off the kitchen opened, and I could hear my mother struggling with the groceries. I quickly put the letters back in the box and went into the living room.

"Are there more in the car?" I asked.

"This is it," she said. "Sorry I'm so late." She put the groceries on the counter and took out orange juice, iceberg lettuce, a store-made rotisserie chicken. "How's this for an early dinner?" she asked.

"Great, but I'm still pretty stuffed from this morning."

"It was a madhouse at Schnucks. You would have thought warheads were on the way," my mother said. "It's Sunday afternoon. I don't understand."

"Everyone's out buying chips and beer," I said. "The Cards are playing a night game and the fans need their fuel."

"Baseball?" she asked.

"Football," I said.

"I thought the football team moved out west."

"They did, but people stay loyal to them anyway. I guess it's all part of the mourning process."

She handed me the latest issue of *Time*. More protests in Eastern Europe. "So what did you do while I was away?"

I leafed absently through the magazine, then set it down. "Not much. Just checked out those old newspapers in the garage. You really don't need to keep them," I said. "We have everything archived at work."

My mother finished unpacking the groceries and leaned against the kitchen sink. "You just want me to throw them away?"

"I assumed you already had."

She looked at me as though we weren't understanding each other, then shook her head and crossed into the living room, gathering up the morning paper. "Those newspapers are your childhood, Gordie," she said, "and I'm going to keep them."

Later that afternoon, we ate our chicken dinner in silence. I had clearly upset her, but I didn't know how nor did I have the energy to set things right again. Reading the letters, I had felt closer to her than I had in months. I had glimpsed a side of my parents' lives that I hadn't known before, but talking about it seemed awkward. Just like that, my mother and I had fallen back into our old patterns.

As I put on my jacket to leave, she was standing in the doorway between the living room and kitchen. "I guess I expect too much," she said, a mix of anger and disappointment in her voice.

"What do you mean?" I turned around to face her.

"I thought we'd have a nice day together, that's all."

"I thought we did," I said, because there was nothing else to say, and crossed the room to hug her goodbye.

10

TUESDAY MARKED two full weeks since Arthur Whiting's funeral, and still I hadn't heard from Alicia. The visit home and my parents' love letters had only increased my loneliness. I had been thinking about driving by Alicia's house again when Arthur's brother, Joe, called me at work.

We had spoken a couple of days after the funeral, right in the middle of deadline, and I'd had to hang up after failing to explain in ten chattery minutes why it was a bad time to talk. He had called back a half-dozen times since, leaving word with the switchboard or, to my great embarrassment, with Ritger, who took a devilish glee in passing on his messages.

"I had a nice talk with your friend Joe Whiting," he'd say, his face a piggish pink. "He's upset you've been stealing his medication."

On the rare occasion that Ritger said something meant to amuse, he'd laugh rapidly through his nose, then stop all of a sudden, letting his face go serious, the way the comedian Paul Lynde used to. But Paul Lynde was funny.

"You're there, perfect, you're there," Joe said, ecstatic that he had finally gotten through. "Right in the nick of time, Nick. You're right in the nick of time."

"Sorry I haven't gotten back to you," I told him, careful not to say too much. "We've been very busy here at the paper. In fact we're very busy now."

The fan above me clattered away. Ritger had gone off to lunch. It was, in reality, the most convenient time for Joe to have called. But I'd set my mind to ignoring him, which was why, when he said something I had waited two weeks to hear, I wasn't listening. Were it not for his manner of catching and repeating certain words, I might not have had another chance to see Alicia.

"I'm going to the museum today," he was saying. "I've been to the museum before. They have pictures on all the walls. Bobby Campanis will be there. The greatest painter of the United States."

I was drawing in blue ink around the outline of Václav Havel's face, the lead picture on the front page of the morning paper. Havel had spoken the night before in front of a huge coalition of opposition groups known as the Civic Forum. Editorials everywhere were predicting that the Czech Communist government would soon fall.

"Margaret won't go because Alicia will be there. You should go. I can give you a ride," Joe was saying. "I don't drive, but I can give you a ride, you know, not me, but the car I'm in can give you a ride."

"It's really not a good time, Joe," I said. "Seriously, I'm going to have to go now."

"Oh, you don't *have* to go. It's not so serious. Don't feel you *have* to go," he said. "Alicia says it's not to be missed. *Not to be missed,* she says."

I sat up.

"What does Alicia have to do with the museum?" I asked.

"Quite a to-do at the museum," he said. "Quite a to-do, and everyone will be there."

I spotted Ritger returning from lunch and hastened Joe Whiting off the phone, thanking him for the call, saying I'd do my best to make it.

I buzzed the research library for a calendar of events and later found an announcement on the schedule for that Tuesday evening, October 22. The announcement must have come from an old press release; Arthur's name was still on it.

> ST. LOUIS DOG MUSEUM — Portrait unveiling of local champion Gambolling Gavin of Galway to be held in the main exhibition room following regular hours at 6 P.M. Featured speakers: Helen Stansbury of Missouri AKA and Arthur Whiting of the Irish Wolfhound Club of North America. Wine and cheese to follow. The dog museum is open to visitors daily, except Mondays and holidays, from 9–5 (Sundays 12–5). A not-for-profit organization.

Driving the back roads to Queeny Park, where the dog museum was located, I wondered if Joe Whiting had called on his own or if Alicia had put him up to it. I tried to imagine that her past two weeks had been as distracting as mine — lingering around the phone, gazing into the mirror, rushing to the window with each footfall on the sidewalk.

I wondered if she hadn't been waiting all this time.

The St. Louis Dog Museum took up the whole of a Greek Revival mansion plus an additional wing, built to meet demand. The lawn, lush and manicured, was dotted with statues of dogs: a pointer at the gate, a Jack Russell along the walk, a basset hound curled in the flower garden, a pair of Saint Bernards guarding the front door.

A woman I recognized from the funeral, the bigger of the two who had sat next to me at the service, was greeting guests. She introduced herself as Mrs. Cunningham. Around her neck was a blue scarf sprinkled with small brown terriers.

"I'm Gordon Hatch. I think we might have met at Arthur Whiting's funeral."

"We're so glad you could come," she said. "It's nice to see you."

She reached around me then, offering a limp hand to someone who had come up behind me. "I see we have the handler, but where is her champion?"

It was Alicia.

She looked lovely, more formal than last I saw her, in a summery off-white linen dress that hung loosely on her body. The puffiness around her eyes had gone. She leaned toward me to shake my hand, a handshake that I could have sworn suggested, *If we were anywhere else I would put my arms around you.*

"I thought you'd come." She smiled in the most casual way, as if we had just seen each other this morning at breakfast. I could feel the blood rushing to my face.

"Gavin isn't feeling well," she told Mrs. Cunningham, "so I've left him at home."

"For his induction?" our greeter asked, somewhat incredulously. "It *must* be serious."

Alicia walked past her, saying she needed to speak with me, and led me from the foyer into the main hall, through a room filled with porcelain Dalmatians and photographs of fire departments posing with their dogs.

"I just needed to take a breath before this all starts," she said. "These little gatherings can drive anybody crazy."

"I was going to call you," I said, feeling more comfortable now. "If you're still interested, I'm more than happy to work on that story we talked about."

"I'm sorry too. I haven't been able to think much about it. I've been packing. I can barely find my feet amidst all of Arthur's things."

At the entrance to the permanent collection, where the addition wing began, she spotted Joe Whiting.

"He's with Bobby Campanis." She nodded in the direction of a man who was listening distractedly to Joe. "You've probably never heard of him — he's not much of a painter, but he does manage to make a living at it, which isn't easy." Her silver bracelets clinked together as she combed her hair around her ears. "I know how hard it is," she said. "I used to be a painter myself."

"You were?" I asked.

"Yes, I did landscapes. I was living in the desert, where you couldn't help but paint."

"Where in the desert?"

"Arizona."

I tumbled this over in my mind for a moment.

"What kind of landscapes?"

She seemed a little embarrassed by the question. "It's hard to summarize. More or less, 'body as landscape, landscape as body,'" she said, as if it were not worth explaining. "But that was a lifetime ago. I haven't picked up a brush in years."

"And what about now?"

"Mostly I've been working with the dogs, grooming and handling, that sort of thing." She shrugged. "But I've already been to the top with Gavin. It's pretty much run its course."

Bobby Campanis was coming up to us now, looking muscular and Mediterranean with a tightly groomed beard that blended smoothly with his cropped black hair. He wore a white T-shirt with black suspenders, tight black pants, and combat boots.

Alicia introduced me as a reporter doing a feature story. Campanis brightened immediately, assuming that the story was about him.

"Mostly I do western scenes," he explained with a New York–New Jersey accent.

He named some painters I'd never heard of — Andrew Melrose, William T. Ranney — and one I knew, George Caleb Bingham, calling them "the dead guys who pay my bills."

He'd been selling his oils on the state fair circuit seventeen years ago — his first trip west of Piscataway — when he was offered a commission by an insurance executive to reproduce *Leaving the Old Homestead,* a James F. Wilkins painting that hung at the Missouri Historical Society.

"Around here it's all about Manifest Destiny," he said. "The people can't get enough of it. Historical stuff, you know. After the Wilkins, there was a Bierstadt, then a Melrose, then boom, I'm in demand."

"Bobby did the picture of Gavin," Joe began excitedly. "Gavin liked getting his picture done. He's a picture dog —"

"That's right, Joe," Alicia said, patting him on the arm to quiet him.

Joe pushed his thick glasses back up his nose, slid his hands into his pockets, and settled into an agitated silence. Alicia's power over him was sweet and impressive.

To be polite, I asked Campanis how he had become interested in dog portraiture. Apparently, Arthur Whiting was to thank for that.

"I did a huge Bingham for the bank he worked at, and he loved it so much he told me, 'One day you're going to have to paint one of my dogs.'"

"Not just a dog. A champion dog," Joe weighed in, stooping his shoulders apologetically.

"Have you painted dogs before?" I asked.

"Oh, sure," Campanis said. "They're always chasing after stage-coaches, plus Daniel Boone had a coonhound. I've probably done a thousand Daniel Boones."

The sound of a gavel was heard from across the room as some-one else I recognized from the funeral took her place beside the portrait, which was covered with a cloth. She wore the same tweed suit from two weeks before.

"First of all, I would like to thank the Ralston Purina Company both for sponsoring this event and for generously commissioning the fine portrait which has brought us together this evening," she said. "Mr. Spears, please take a bow."

Applause rose from the audience of no more than forty people, and the youthful Mr. Spears half stood, waving from the front row, where folding chairs had been set up around a lectern.

"Also, this event could not have taken place without the efforts of Evelyn Cunningham and Barbara Moore Seawickly, co-chairpersons of the Sight Hound Club of Middle America."

The big woman at the front door and her friend acknowledged the light applause by standing up in different parts of the room and clapping in each other's direction, to indicate, *The credit is all yours.*

"I'm Helen Stansbury, curator of the St. Louis Dog Museum, and I'd like to welcome you all to this grand occasion. Today we recognize not only a great local champion but a dog of national prominence — winner in Lubbock of Best of Breed at the tender age of fourteen months; winner in the Hound Division at the Steel City Kennel Club six months later; winner of Best in Show at Louisville, October 1988; and at two and a half, winner of Best of Breed and Best in the Sight Hound Division at the one hundred twelfth Westminster Kennel Club show in New York City."

She looked up at the audience, taking off her glasses and setting them on the lectern.

"Gambolling Gavin of Galway is the youngest dog ever to have his portrait hung on these museum walls. He is the most distinguished St. Louis champion since the pug Calypso Mirabella, owned by Mr. Herbert Etheridge of Creve Coeur, who is here with us today."

A fist rose from the middle of the room and shook in the air.

"As many of you know, this event is bittersweet," Ms. Stansbury continued. "Gavin's owner, Arthur Whiting, passed away suddenly three weeks ago and in the prime of life. Mr. Whiting was editor of the *Irish Wolfhound Quarterly,* majority owner of the Mississippi Valley Irish Wolfhound Farm, an active member of the board of this museum, and a regular contributor to a number of hound club newsletters. He was one of the most committed members of the show dog community, and his loss will be deeply felt." There was a hush as people turned to look sympathetically at Alicia.

She was standing beside me, her arm trembling against mine. I wanted to touch her shoulder, reassure her.

The museum curator wrapped up her speech and brought Bobby Campanis before the audience, where he was warmly received. He said a few words about how well behaved Gavin was, how he had sat for his portrait barely moving for the whole eight hours.

"I've got a golden retriever," he said. "You wanna talk about ants in the pants."

When the cloth was lifted, there was a unanimous "Ahh." People got up from their seats and gathered around the portrait for a closer look: on a high bluff over a wide river Gavin sat nobly surveying a dark and ominous landscape. A beam of sunlight fell from above. His masters, a woman in a white veil and a man with a musket slung over his shoulder, stood behind him. A single gnarled tree seemed to point across the river to the open prairie on the other side.

"See, look what I told you," Joe said. "He's the best. So true to life. Totally lifelike. As true as life can be —"

Alicia politely lifted a finger to her lips. "It's just gorgeous, Bobby," she said with the appropriate amount of conviction.

As wine and hors d'oeuvres were brought around, Alicia and I managed to find a corner in the back of the room to talk.

"This must be nice for you," I said, leaning against the wall, trying to look casual, a glass of wine held next to my cheek. "Even if the painting isn't so good, it must be an honor to have Gavin's portrait in this museum."

"Oh, I don't know," she sighed. "This is Arthur's world, and the people in it are a lot older than me." She rubbed her hands over her arms as if she were getting cold. "I never missed a single dog show in the entire time that Arthur and I were together. I was completely devoted, and he used to give me all the credit for Gavin's success. But he was the only one. Most of the people here don't even like me."

I had assumed these people were her friends, but she did seem out of place in this crowd.

"Packing up the last couple of weeks, I've realized how poorly I fit this group. I even look odd in the photographs," she said. "I have no problem with a little snobbery so long as there's an intelligence behind it. But these people aren't smart or ambitious; they're just exclusive." The light on her skin was warm and inviting. "Arthur's death has made me see that I want to do something else with my life. This just isn't my world anymore."

Soon we were joined by Mrs. Cunningham, a plate of crackers in hand. Alicia thanked her for the evening and asked if she knew whether Joe had a ride home.

"He came with the painter," Mrs. Cunningham said. "An interesting fellow, that Campanis, and quite an outfit he's wearing too." She raised her eyebrow sardonically. "The two of them make quite a pair."

Then it was Mrs. Seawickly at our side. Somehow she had found a Scotch on the rocks at this wine and cheese party. "Am I missing something?" she asked. "I heard laughter."

"I was just telling Alicia how nice it is that her brother-in-law has found a friend," Mrs. Cunningham addressed the smaller woman, pulling lightly at her dog scarf. "I imagine life for Joe is awfully lonely, out on that farm with nobody to talk to but the wolfhounds. But I hear wolfhounds are the finest listeners among the *Canis familiaris*." She laughed as they walked away.

Alicia looked at me, rolling her eyes as if to say, *Why even bother?*

"Isn't that your sister-in-law?" I asked.

Helen Stansbury was talking to Margaret Whiting, who seemed to be scanning the room. Nearly a head taller than everyone else, Margaret looked distinctly preoccupied.

Alicia set her wine on a nearby table. "That it is. Let's go," she said, brushing my hand. "This is too much."

"Where?" Was she inviting me along?

"It would be nice if I could talk to a real person for a change.

Have a real conversation. You don't mind, do you?" I'd never had much practice reading women's expressions, but for all I knew, the downward turn of her mouth held promise.

"Where?" I asked again, too quickly.

"Well, I really should do some more packing. How about my house? Why don't you follow my car."

We left without saying goodbye to anyone. On the way out of the back room, Alicia kept looking over toward Margaret, who still seemed not to have noticed us.

"She'll never forgive me for marrying her brother," Alicia said as she climbed hurriedly into her Delta 88. By the time I had started the Gremlin, she was already pulling out of the dog museum driveway.

I had to drive like mad to keep up with her. She must have been going 50 in a 25-mile-per-hour zone, forcing me to fly through two yellow lights and a red before I caught up at the turnoff to two-laned Highway 40. Out on the highway she passed a slow-moving carpet truck, but I was caught in the right-hand lane. One car after the next whooshed past me on the left.

The Gremlin begins to shake at 60 miles per hour, so I sat in the slow lane, the needle stuck on 52, pounding my fist on the dash-board, fuming at the cartoon figure of a genie emerging from a bottle painted on the back of the carpet truck, with the message "You Can't Wish for Lower Prices."

When the left-hand lane finally cleared, I saw Alicia's car, a stripe of blue sinking over the horizon.

Turning off the highway onto the 270 loop, I began to calm down. I knew where she lived. I didn't need to follow her. I could simply meet her there. But when I took the familiar turn off Kingshighway onto Dalecarlia and looked for the blue Delta 88 in the driveway, it had not arrived.

I pulled up in front, cut the engine, and waited. Seven-thirty. The sun was long gone, the last light of dusk about to fade. Perhaps she had stopped at a liquor store to buy some wine. I waited five minutes, then ten, then half an hour. Maybe she had been hungry and had gone to a pizza place or somewhere else along the way to pick up dinner.

Then I began to worry that something might have happened to her. A flat tire. Engine trouble. The way she was driving, she could have had an accident.

The streetlight in front of Alicia's house was out, and before long I was sitting in complete darkness, watching in my rear-view mirror for her car to turn onto the street.

11

LATER THAT NIGHT I called her, pressing Redial every thirty seconds, pacing the apartment. I turned the scanner on low, listening
for accidents. I thought about calling Holman to see if he had
heard of any crashes on the highway.

I imagined visiting her at the hospital, bandaged, stabilized, surrounded by tubes. I'd bring her flowers and books and newspapers, keep her from sinking into total despair. I'd stay with her every night on a cot in her room in the ICU, then move into the
guest room on Dalecarlia Drive when she was ready to go home.
She'd have to learn to walk again; rehab would take more than a
year; every day she'd want to give up. In the end, she'd tell all of our
friends that I saved her life.

When I finally reached her, she sounded drowsy.

"It's Gordon Hatch," I said. "I thought we were going to meet at
your house. I must have lost you."

Alicia perked up. "Where were *you*? I thought you were right behind me. What happened?"

"I was following you for a while until I got stuck in the slow
lane. I looked up and you were gone," I said. "My car's pretty old. It
doesn't do so hot on the highway."

"Well, there was definitely somebody following me. I thought it was you," she said. "I stopped at the Zebra Room. They've got little jukeboxes at all the tables. I thought we'd have a drink first."

I felt a flutter of excitement at the word "first," whatever "first" meant. We'd have a drink "first," and then what? I stood up with the phone and walked the perimeter of the throw rug in my living room.

"Should we try again tomorrow night?" I asked. "I've never been to the Zebra Room. I'd love to see it. Those jukeboxes —"

"Great jukeboxes," she said. "I love that about St. Louis. There are a lot of authentic bars, the kind that were actually built in the forties and fifties rather than just made to look that way."

"What time should we meet?" I was surprised by my own boldness.

"I'll go to the Zebra Room, sure," she said. "I've got the appraiser coming in at six. They serve great pizza. We can get a pizza and then go out somewhere."

All morning at work I replayed this conversation in my head for clues as to how the night would go. She had as much as invited me to her house. I made a mental collage of her willing looks: smiling when I kissed her hand, brushing against me as we left the museum, looks that ordinarily would have paralyzed a man like me.

Late in the morning, Thea called.

"Let's do something," she said. "I have the afternoon off."

"How did you manage that?"

"I think they're worried I'll collapse on them. I've been sleeping in chairs for the last four days."

"Then take a nap. Don't be ridiculous."

"I'm fine," she said. "Honestly. I'd really like to catch up with you. There's a lot going on."

We agreed to meet for lunch at an Italian place near the *Independent*.

Thea was leaning over the bar drinking a Diet Coke when I

walked into the restaurant. I tapped her on the shoulder and she swiveled around, biting her lip. Her skin was unhealthy, the color of metal, her hair pulled back in a long ponytail. She wore faded jeans and leather sandals and a white T-shirt with "St. Louis" and "University" curving around a red caduceus.

"Don't be overwhelmed by my beauty," she said. "It's only a temporary thing."

She slid off the bar stool and hugged me. I hadn't remembered her being quite so tall.

In our booth toward the back of the restaurant, she asked me about my job and I was vague in answering. I said I was busy with a number of assignments, some of them confidential, and that I was still at the obituary desk. I talked about my difficulties with Ritger and St. John and told her what my mother used to say, that I had a poor temperament for responding to authority. I went on for a while about the job, bringing up my father, who had never worked for small-minded men, having shot to the top so quickly. I was tempted to tell her about Alicia, but I checked myself.

Thea said that she'd been thinking about her father too; he'd recently been out visiting.

"Everything is different now," she said. "I wanted to tell you as soon as it happened, but not on the telephone." She paused. "On Sunday, as he was leaving to go back to Columbia, my father had a heart attack." She was sliding her fingers along the edge of the table. "He's in Intensive Care at the VA Hospital."

I suddenly felt weak, as happens with bad news. I wanted to say the right thing, even, simply, "I'm so sorry, Thea," but instead I sat there speechless.

When the waitress came by with menus, I opened mine, to fill the space, then felt embarrassed to be holding it.

"A few months ago he had a silent heart attack," Thea said. "A portion of the heart muscle died, and a thin scar formed in its place."

"That's really awful." My eyes were fixed on the daily special, eggplant parmigiana, $5.95 with a house salad. I couldn't stand eggplant.

"The scar wasn't strong enough to contain the pressure of heart contractions, so he developed an aneurysm. It's like a sac bulging outward with every beat." She demonstrated with her hands. "The aneurysm was making the heart overcompensate."

Too distracted to focus, I had only a gauzy sense of Thea's father, tall and narrow with a rocking gait. I tried to listen, telling myself that Thea was once everything to me.

The waitress returned, and Thea ordered a cup of minestrone.

"That's it?" I asked. "You've got to eat."

"I'm really not hungry," she said. "I haven't had an appetite."

"I'll have the chicken sandwich," I said to the waitress, handing her my menu.

She opened the menu, placing it back in front of me. "This is Italian food, honey. We don't do a chicken sandwich. You can try the chicken parmigiana or the chicken florentine — "

"I'll have the special," I blurted out.

"Eggplant?" she asked.

"Fine." My face flushed.

I found myself watching Thea's hands as they skimmed along the surface of the table, rising to make a point or to demonstrate a medical procedure.

"When they removed the aneurysm, they sewed in a shunt," she said. "The success rate is pretty high, but a lot can go wrong."

I thought of when I had known her so well, never noticing these square hands, small-fingered, wonderfully wrinkled around the joints. I felt myself staring, had the sense that I must have looked odd sitting there as distracted as I was, every expression somehow wrong.

But Thea seemed not to notice. She continued to detail her father's condition, as though finding a kind of comfort in the sterile language of medicine.

"Well, it's so lucky that we live in the same town," she concluded as the waitress brought our food. I jabbed at the eggplant, a sponge slathered in tomato sauce.

"My other friends are too young. Nothing has ever happened to them. It makes them nervous to talk about sickness or death," she said. "But you understand because of your father."

"I didn't really know my father," I reminded her. "He was dead by the time I was five." I pushed my plate aside. "My father is really a collection of my mother's stories."

It occurred to me that this was something new. I hadn't thought about it that way — the words had just come out — but somehow what I had said felt like a truth.

"I remembered that he worked in Chicago," Thea said. "I took a tour of the *Tribune* once and tried to get his articles for you, but the guide told me that it couldn't be done."

"Not unless you work there," I guessed. "It's company policy a lot of places."

"But *you* must have a way of getting them," Thea said.

She was right, of course. I could have gotten them. My father's clips were a library request away, a few punches on the keyboard and up they would come: ten years on the fronts of history. My mother had never shown me the clips and I had never asked. My assumption was that one day we'd sit in the living room and spread them all out and read them one by one over a long, rainy weekend. When I had made it, when I had truly arrived as a journalist, she would open the rolltop desk and I would know everything.

After lunch I walked with Thea to the bus stop. It was getting colder. The sky was darkening. By the time we got there, a drizzle had begun to fall.

"It was nice to see you again." I rolled down my sleeves. "I'm very sorry about your father. Let me know if there's anything I can do."

She nodded and embraced me, lightly, as if one of us were breakable, saying, "Thank you, Gordie. Next time you see me I promise I'll wash my hair." She laughed, stepping into the shelter beside the bus stop.

On the walk back to the *Independent,* a cold wind blew up and the drizzle became rain. I crossed my arms, pulling in my shoulders, turned off Locust to Seventh Street. For three o'clock on a Wednesday afternoon, downtown St. Louis was desolate — nothing but gray buildings with dark lobbies, empty sports bars and greeting card shops. Seventh Street stopped at Busch Stadium, where, a month before, baseball season had ended. Without any people, without the bright colors and the movement of fans filing in, it was a lifeless concrete bowl.

The Zebra Room was a quarter mile down the same road in St. Charles as Crawley's Funeral Home, in the first block of a recently gentrified stretch of upmarket shops and chain stores. It sat at the front of a brand-new parking lot, a brightly lit relic from the soda shop days, made of red tile and chrome with a long zebra-striped awning reaching out toward the main road.

Inside, the place was crowded, a curious mix of older couples who smoked and looked out the window and upper-income families of four in bright polo shirts. The hostess said it would be a half hour before a table was ready. Alicia had not yet arrived, so I put my name on the list and waited outside.

The rain had stopped, and the parking lot asphalt drew water into its pores with a hiss. I slouched against a pole at the end of the awning, picturing myself from the road where Alicia would soon be turning, my posture under the streetlights out of film noir.

"This place has certainly been discovered," she said, walking out of the darkness into my line of vision. She must have used some other entrance to the parking lot. "Have you been here long?"

"I just got here," I said, though it had been twenty minutes. "Our name's on the list."

"I can't stand it when places I like get discovered. Last night was okay, but this is ridiculous. Look at them all pressed in there."

She was in blue jeans and sneakers and a white cotton sweater. Anyone seeing us together would have thought we were the same age.

"How long is the wait?" she asked.

"No more than ten or fifteen minutes."

"That's too long. Let's go to my house," she said, touching the sleeve of my pullover rain jacket. "It's kind of a mess, but I've been to the grocery today. Do you like stir-fry?"

"Sure I like stir-fry." A current of anticipation rolled over my ribs as I began to think that it *was* me she was interested in, not the article on Arthur.

"I've got *Fanny and Alexander*. Have you seen it?"

Thea and I had rented it once, giving up after the first cassette of crazy uncles making jokes that didn't translate, dinner parties at long, abundant tables, and, ultimately, unhappiness.

"I've heard it's his most brilliant film," I said. "I'd love to see it."

This time I kept up with Alicia's driving, following her for a couple of miles to Dalecarlia and Kingshighway.

She must have known that the Zebra Room would be crowded; she'd been there the night before, after all. I had the feeling, catching a glimpse of myself in the rear-view mirror as we turned onto her street, that Alicia had done this all quite deliberately: the groceries, the video, the crowded restaurant. My certainty that this was the night gave me a rare confidence.

Her house was a mess, but there was something romantic about a house in transition. She brought tablecloths and blankets from a dining room cupboard and a couple of throws from an old Army chest, and we draped them over the boxes cluttering her living room.

The living room was dark, lit by a single floor lamp next to the hard Victorian couch that sat in her bay window. Loose trinkets — a silver snuffer, porcelain dogs, a cherub figurine plucking a harp — lay around the coffee table. All the pictures were down from the walls, leaning against the fireplace, the one in front a watercolor of the houses of parliament seen from across the Thames.

"I'm sorry about the state of the place," Alicia said. "I'm getting ready to move."

Newspapers and packing tape and bubble wrap were strewn on the floor. She gathered the newspapers into a pile, dropping them in a grapefruit box.

"It's charming." I popped a few cells of bubble wrap. "Almost gothic if you had some candles and spider webs."

"I do have candles, lots of them." She walked to the dining room, opened a box, and unwrapped a few three-pronged candlesticks and candles. She placed the candlesticks on top of boxes around the room, then went to the kitchen and lit one of the candles from her gas stove, dipping it wick to wick so that soon the whole room was flickering with candlelight and shadows.

I was amazed that she had taken what I'd said and made something beautiful of it.

Alicia herself seemed in transition. She was more optimistic than before, even happy, like someone anticipating her future.

"You do the rice and I'll chop," she said, opening a bottle of white wine and pouring us each a glass.

Her kitchen, small and cramped, had for the most part yet to be packed away — more evidence, I assumed, that she had been planning to bring me here all along.

When the water came to a boil and I had put the lid on the rice to let it simmer, I leaned forward on the counter, and asked, "What else?"

She pointed with her long knife toward a cabinet over the refrigerator, where I found sesame oil and soy sauce. "I haven't done stir-fry in a long time," she said. "Mostly I bake. But lately I've realized I'm not fond of baking."

I didn't have much to add on the subject — my mother and I were microwave chefs — but I did like the fresh scent of chopped vegetables and the spit of the hot skillet, the oily humidity in the room, the salt rising and settling on my skin.

Alicia pushed the onions around with a wooden spoon.

"You could cut the mushrooms," she said.

She added red and green peppers, chopped garlic, thin strips of chicken.

I sliced the mushrooms thick, lightly touching her arm with the cutting board as I handed it to her.

"Thank you," she said with a small smile.

Since the dining room table was covered with files and papers and photograph albums, we put our plates on top of one of the long cardboard boxes in the living room. I turned off the standing lamp by the window and Alicia set two votive candles between our plates.

She poured what remained of the wine, filling my glass almost to the top.

"What should we toast?" I asked.

Alicia sat cross-legged on the floor. I sat sideways, my legs swung out.

"I'm not sure," she said. "You tell me."

Her eyes reflected the gold flickering of the candlelight, the obscured outline of my own face across the makeshift table.

"To finding a nice place for all these boxes," I said.

After we finished eating, we opened a second bottle of wine and lay on our backs on either side of the long packing box. Blades of shadow intersected on the walls.

"I want a house with higher ceilings," Alicia was saying. "Low ceilings close me in."

"I'd like to own a lodge." I turned my head to look at her. "A lodge at the base of some mountain out west with a huge stone fireplace, old skis and snowshoes and bear heads along the walls."

"I like bears," she said, sitting up, suddenly blowing out the votives. "Should we watch the movie now?"

I followed her through the kitchen to the other half of the

house, where she led me by the hand into her and Arthur's bedroom.

I thought she might kiss me. We were that close.

The bedroom had blue-bordered wallpaper, heavy furniture, and shag carpeting. Flattened boxes leaned against the closet door. Packed boxes were lined up next to the bed, a four-poster with a lace canopy and small steps climbing up one side. Atop a stack of framed photographs was a picture of Alicia and her wolfhound at one of the dog shows.

"Where is Gavin anyway?" I asked. I hadn't even thought about the dog.

Alicia was standing in front of the television screen, fast-forwarding through the trailers. "He's still not feeling well. I put him out back in the dog run. The fresh air should help."

As the film began, she turned off the overhead light and climbed onto the bed, patting a place beside her. "You can sit with me," she said.

I stood by the side of her bed, dizzy with desire.

"Quite an elaborate bed. I'll have to take the stairs," I managed, and she laughed.

Theoretically, I supposed, she was still a married woman. It hadn't been a month since Arthur had died, after all, but I was trying not to think about that. Alicia covered her smile with the back of her hand, sliding over to make room, handing me three pillows. Her bed was full of pillows.

Fanny and Alexander begins on Christmas Eve; the family estate is festooned in red — red drapes in all the windows, red bows on the Christmas tree, the chairs upholstered in red, red curtains hanging along the walls, the matron of the house giving orders in a red velvet dress. The film gave Alicia's bedroom a warm red glow.

I paid very little attention to the film, tuning in occasionally to read subtitles when Alicia responded to something. Instead I watched her feet, her thin ankles. She had remarkably thin ankles.

My thumb and middle finger could have wrapped around them and touched..My leg brushed her leg as I shifted, and she didn't move away.

She seemed to watch with detached interest, wiggling her feet, shifting every so often.

The family and servants in the film held hands and danced through the house singing Christmas songs in Swedish. I felt remarkably at ease, prepared by days of imagining this moment. I thought about winter, blankets on the bed, hot drinks, coming in from the cold. At Christmas we'd exchange presents. I'd bring Alicia home and my mother would love her straightaway.

Alicia sat up with a start. "Was that the doorbell?" She crawled across the bed and pressed Pause on the VCR.

"I didn't hear anything." Actually, I had heard something but assumed it was from the movie.

"I'm going to check the door," she said.

I made a move to join her, but she waved me back. "I'll just be a minute."

A moment later she was back, shutting the door behind her.

"Well?" I asked.

"It was Margaret." Alicia shook her head.

"What did she want?" It was ten o'clock at night.

"Who knows? I wasn't about to answer it." She climbed back into the bed, fixing the pillows. "Margaret used to live here, you know. She's always lurking around."

"She used to live here?" I was surprised.

"Long story," Alicia said. "Let's put the movie back on."

I pressed the play button, climbed the steps back into bed, and lay down beside her.

"You're sweet," she said, and turned and kissed my cheek, sliding her leg over mine, her knee between my knees. She put her hand over my palm and I grasped it, weaving her fingers through mine. We rolled onto our sides, facing each other. Her eyes were closed as our mouths came together. With her fingers she traced my jawline, unbuttoned my shirt, eased my pants over my hips. When she sat up and pulled off her sweater, her body was bathed in a cathode red.

In the swoon between consciousness and sleep, that middle place where things seem clear, I had a dream that may well not have been a dream but a memory. I'm two, three, four years old, walking across the slick gray tile of a locker room shower into the stark brightness of a public swimming pool. The midsummer heat is infused with chlorine and the excited screams of children splashing about, padding along the deck.

It's a small town, like many of the small towns I'd driven through as a child, only this swimming pool sits in the middle of the town square and is fed by a towering, twisting blue waterslide.

From the shallow end I watch the children at the other end of the pool climb the high ladder to the top of the waterslide, silhouetted against a pharmacy, hardware store, and five-and-dime. They go down head first, feet first — Superman, toboggan. The bold ones get a running start.

I watch them longingly.

Two hands reach under my arms and lift me up. I'm swept into the air and when my feet come down they're touching water. First step. Second step. I'm lifted, gently pushed until the water is waist high, until it's up to my chin.

Out of instinct, my legs start kicking. The hands move under my belly, large hands that could cover me completely or swallow me up.

The shallow end is empty except for a woman ahead of us in a black bathing cap, who faces away, leaning her elbows over the lip of the pool.

I kick and paddle my arms. The hands beneath me become ten fingers, then six, then two, then none at all.

The children's laughter goes quiet, tinny, as my ears drop below the surface.

Ahead of me, the woman in the bathing cap turns and smiles. White arms, dark eyes. She reaches out to receive me.

I stop kicking and paddling and let myself sink beneath the surface, and as the world disappears, I wait for the large hands to reach under my arms and lift me up again.

I awoke to a scream.

"What was that?"

"What?" Alicia asked. She was sitting up in bed watching the movie, wearing my oxford shirt, unbuttoned.

"That scream," I said, and heard it again, this time longer than the first, more guttural.

Alicia laughed, leaning over to kiss me. "Poor boy," she said.

The scream had come from the television set, where the two children, Fanny and Alexander, were wandering through the hallways of their great family house, awakened in the middle of the night by the same screams that had awoken me. The screams grew louder, more frequent, as the children followed them to their source.

Through the crack of a half-opened door, Fanny and Alexander watched a woman pacing in front of the open coffin of an older man, her long, wounded screams filling the night.

"What happened?" I asked.

"Their father died," Alicia said.

"How?"

"He just died. I'm not sure."

She ran her fingers from the back of my head through my hair. Thin fingers with long fingernails.

"And that's his wife?"

"Yes, that's his wife."

"She's pretty," I said, reaching my arm behind Alicia's waist, curling myself around her. "Not as pretty as you."

❖ 12 ❖

THOSE FIRST DAYS, I barely slept.

I'd hold her hand all night and try to stay still and open my eyes at dawn to watch her, bare-shouldered, peaceful beside me. She called me "sweetheart." Almost immediately, she called me "sweetheart." So soon. We were that comfortable. That easy together.

This was Alicia's gift. I dropped my guard.

My father's life fascinated her. She wanted to know everything about him, to the point where I'd call my mother from the office to collect further anecdotes and fill out his career. I told her about the Kennedy assassination, the Warren Commission investigation and the Jack Ruby trial, my father's two-year stint in Dallas, first with the *Kansan,* then later with the *Chicago Tribune.*

Alicia was from Dallas. Her father, it turned out, had been a career police officer in Fort Worth, a member of the security detail at the Fort Worth airport that sunny morning when the President boarded his short flight from Fort Worth to Dallas's Love Field. Alicia's father had seen Kennedy board the plane. My father had seen him disembark. I cherished this connection between us.

In 1965, my father moved to Chicago to run the *Tribune*'s city desk. For three turbulent years he took on Mayor Daley's political machine, jumping from editor to columnist before becoming lead reporter for the 1968 election. He sat in the front row of the White House press room when, at the end of a dull Sunday press conference, Lyndon Johnson surprised the world with an announcement: "I shall not seek, and I will not accept, the nomination of my party for another term as your President." And when Bobby Kennedy was killed in California, my father was following the Wallace campaign through the Deep South.

"It's probably good he wasn't in L.A.," Alicia said. "You can only distance yourself so much from something so horrible."

I had never felt such an intensity of interest from anyone, not even Thea. I'd always followed my passions alone, but now, with someone to share them, I felt edgy, invulnerable.

I told her about the '68 Democratic Convention, when my father had his head bloodied by Chicago police. Mayor Daley had refused to issue a permit to a group of young war demonstrators led by what would later be known as the Chicago Seven. The blue-helmeted police force waded into packed crowds, thrashing protesters and onlookers with impunity, injuring hundreds.

My father never forgave Mayor Daley for the scar on his head. Promoted after the election to managing editor, he relentlessly attacked Daley's tolerance of local corruption and his questionable use of power.

In the middle of our first week together, Alicia planned an estate sale for the coming Saturday, the second day of November. The weather was beginning to turn, and she wanted to take advantage of what was supposed to be a warm weekend.

I was secretly pleased that so many of Arthur's possessions would be sold. The sooner Alicia moved on, I figured, the more open our future would be. I helped with the packing, labeling, and pricing of Arthur's things, and she resisted telling me the history of each artifact. I couldn't bear to think that she had lived a separate life before me, that another man had slept in her bed, kept his razor in her medicine cabinet, bought her gifts. I knew one thing

about myself from my experience with Thea: I was a deeply jealous person.

That Friday, to my surprise, I got a call at the office from Margaret
Whiting.

"I had been thinking about calling you, but then Joe told me he
saw you at the dog museum," she said, implying some kind of dis-
loyalty.

It was a curious way to begin a conversation, but I rolled with it.
"I was there because Joe invited me. He seemed eager for me to
meet his painter friend. It was a nice evening."

"Why didn't I see you?" she asked. "I was there as well."

"I must have blended with the crowd." I recalled the event's
modest attendance.

"So what about this story you're writing on my brother? I assume that's another reason you were there."

I had frankly forgotten about the story, which now seemed absurd, as I was attempting to remove all traces of Arthur Whiting.

"Perhaps we can talk about it," I said. "I assume you'll be at the
estate sale?"

"What estate sale?" she asked.

And before I could catch myself, recognizing my mistake even as
I was speaking the words, I heard myself say, "Arthur's things are
being put up for sale tomorrow."

"Oh," she sighed, sounding bewildered. "I hadn't heard about
that."

I thought about Margaret ringing the doorbell while Alicia and
I were watching the movie the other night, how perhaps she had
still been waiting outside as we lay in bed together. And I wondered why I was hearing from her now.

"Alicia will be awfully surprised to see me there," Margaret said.

"Are you sure you wouldn't rather meet somewhere else?" I
asked.

"No, we'll meet at the estate sale," she said. "Don't worry about your own skin. I'll tell her I saw it advertised in the paper."

Next to Alicia's bedroom there was a small guest room done in pink wallpaper, where by Saturday morning we had moved all the boxes and pieces of furniture that weren't being put up for sale. It surprised me how little she planned to take with her: five boxes, three suitcases, a leather portfolio, a couple of hanging bags, a folding bookshelf, a radio and cassette player — no more than could fit in her car. I loved how she traveled light, needed little, had the strength to pick up and start again. My mother had done the same after my father died. She knew she couldn't bear to remain in Chicago, so she packed up the house, leaving nearly everything behind.

Alicia and I spent all morning cleaning. I mowed the lawn, clipped the hedges, raked the leaves into bags, and put a bowl of water out for Gavin, who eyed me suspiciously. Alicia swept and dusted and cleaned off the tabletops, bought cut flowers and placed them in all the rooms. Late in the morning, as I was carrying a pumpkin from the kitchen to the front stoop, she followed me outside.

"Do you think it's strange?" she asked.

"To have an estate sale? People do this all the time."

"That's not what I'm asking. Do you think it's strange that I can love you so soon after Arthur?"

Her question took me aback. The thought had crossed my mind, but I'd been trying not to dwell on it. I put the pumpkin down.

"You don't have to say anything, Gordie. I know it's a little odd." Her hands were still caked with the batter of the zucchini bread she was baking. She had said earlier that estate sales didn't need to be somber; she had heard somewhere that the best way to sell anything is to bake three loaves of bread and put Vivaldi in the tape deck. "I adored my husband, but certain aspects of me he refused to understand." She rolled the dough off her fingers, pinching it into a ball. "You're not like that. You take things as they come."

Shortly before noon, when the estate sale was advertised to begin, Alicia slipped *Stabat Mater* into the cassette player, opened the front door to the house, and led me to the shower off the master bedroom, pressing her small high breasts against my dirty shirt.

I stripped, leaving my clothes in the half-open bathroom doorway.

She worked the soap into a lather in her hands and washed the grass and dirt I had brought in from the yard off my legs and arms, massaged her sweet-scented shampoo into my scalp, standing me under the running water so we were belly to belly.

Afterward, Alicia dried herself off and walked in a towel to her closet, where she dressed. My change of clothes was in the pink room. I'd have to cross the master bedroom to get there. Over the music, I couldn't tell if anyone had arrived.

I ducked my head and walked quickly through the hallway to the pink room, shutting the door behind me. At a glance I'd seen that the hallway was empty. Careless. But this was how it went with me and Alicia.

I dried my hair and put on a fresh pair of khakis and a white shirt, opening one of Alicia's boxes so I could hide the clothes I'd worn in the morning in case Margaret came looking around this room. The box was marked "Letters." Near the top was a stack of bound notebooks, and the first one, written in a scrawl that was unmistakably Alicia's, was labeled

JOURNAL
NO. 23
MARCH 1988–JANUARY 1989

I was tempted to open it, quickly read an entry or two, but I resisted. Instead, I moved my clothes into the "Sweaters" box nearby.

*   *   *

Alicia was in the living room showing a young couple the Victorian couch.

"So, what is it you do?" the man asked Alicia, now in blue jeans and a T-shirt. Her hair was up in a bun with a pencil stuck through it. I wanted to stand beside her as she greeted people, put my arm over her shoulder, have her introduce me proprietarily, but instead I browsed the room as if I were just another buyer looking at the merchandise.

"I'm between jobs, actually," she said. "I had thought for a while about veterinary school, but five years is an awfully long time. Lately I'm interested in newspaper reporting."

"That's quite a switch," the man said. "How interesting."

"I don't want to go to school for it." Alicia leaned against the arm of the couch. "The best school of journalism is getting in there and doing it."

The words were exactly as I had spoken them to her.

"Good reporters have the luck of oil men," she said. "The story seems always to be just beneath their feet."

I was turning the bust of a headless Roman-looking figure around in my hands when Alicia called me over.

"This is a journalist friend of mine, Gordie Hatch. He works at the *St. Louis Independent*."

I shook hands with the couple.

"You might know a friend of mine, Marshall Holman," the man said. "I played football with him at Illinois."

"Sure, I know Marshall. He's one of our police reporters."

"Great guy. Damn funny guy." The man looked small to have played Division I football, with a neck no larger than mine. Maybe he was the kicker, I thought, or an overachieving walk-on.

"Marshall red-shirted his freshman year, then quit," he continued. "Strangest thing, because he was highly recruited." The man's wife smiled at him proudly. He obviously loved telling football stories. "He said he'd never be fast enough for the pro game, so he gave up his scholarship and started working for the Champaign paper."

Alicia had stepped away and now returned with two cups of coffee.

"What do you do at the *Independent*?" the man asked, taking a sip.

I looked at Alicia, with whom I'd not been entirely honest concerning the state of my career, and she smiled, a smile remarkably similar to that of the woman whose husband told his football story.

"I'm with the metro section. I do this and that, mostly general assignment work."

"You said your name is Hatch? I always read Metro. Best section in the paper, if you want my opinion."

So he wouldn't press me any further, I sat on the couch, bouncing on it a little. "Comfortable," I said. "How much for this piece?"

Alicia gave me a disappointed look. "He's so modest. He hates talking about himself. The truth is, Gordie's an investigative reporter, so you only see his articles a few times a year. But they're always blockbusters — five- and six-part series, the kind that get picked up nationally."

"Really?" the man said. "I love those investigative series. Which ones have you done?"

I named two recent series that the *Independent* had run, one about fraud surrounding the proposed riverboat casinos and the other, sanctioned by St. John, about a crack-addicted investment broker leading a double life.

"Oh yeah, I remember that second one," the football player said. "Tragic story, especially the part where his wife's giving birth and he's in the hospital bathroom getting loaded."

I shook my head, lifting the floor lamp to check its price tag. "Twenty-five dollars. That's a bargain," I said. "Can you set this one aside for me?"

As the living room filled with people, I left Alicia and the couple and went back to browsing.

Leaning against the wall were the paintings that before had been stacked next to the fireplace. There were five in all: the houses of parliament watercolor; a realistic still life of a bowl of fruit; a group of pelican-like birds, taken, I guessed, from an old zoological textbook; another watercolor of a wagon wheel in a field; plus a triptych that next to these others seemed incongruous: a reclining nude divided into three parts — head, torso, legs.

The first four paintings didn't interest me — I would have guessed that they were copies — but the nude was striking. Earlier in the day when Alicia had set it against the wall I had only glanced at it, noticing that it was larger in size and brighter than the rest. But now, something about the glassy, lifeless stare in the nude's eyes, her remarkably real flesh tones, the vibrant, almost pulsating fire-orange background, fascinated me.

"Do you think we could save this?" I asked Alicia on her way into the kitchen.

"Why that one?"

"I don't know. I like it," I said. "I can tell you it's worth a lot more than fifty dollars."

Alicia shrugged her shoulders. "If you want it, sure." She handed me three Sold stickers. I carried the painting in three trips to the pink room.

Margaret was outside on the patio. She must not have come through the house or I would have seen her.

"You're here," I said stupidly, because even though I had known she was coming, I was still unnerved.

She stood beside the fenced-in dog run. Joe was inside it, sitting on the packed dirt, nuzzling Gavin.

"Did you have to drive far?" I asked.

"I live less than a mile from here" was her curt reply.

I waved to Joe, and he nodded, stroking Gavin's face.

"Can I get you something to eat?" I asked Margaret. "I saw some zucchini bread and coffee in the kitchen."

"That would be nice." She was pulling dead blooms off the rhododendrons that grew alongside the dog run, stuffing them into her pocket. "Maybe a cup of coffee, black, and a piece of plain toast."

In the kitchen, Alicia was making a fresh pot.

"You can't be so shy with people," she said, rubbing my back. "You're an excellent reporter at one of the best papers in the country. Why diminish yourself?"

I put two pieces of bread in the toaster oven and took two cups off the shelf.

"Seriously, sweetheart. You have to get over this shyness."

"You're right," I said. "I'm just not used to telling people what I do."

The fact was, in the year since I'd moved to St. Louis I had met almost no one, had had no social life to speak of. My whole existence had been work and advancers.

"It's simple," she said. "You're an investigative reporter. Your articles come out only a few times a year. If they want to know more than that, you say, 'Sorry, I have to keep things quiet until we break the story.'"

With a quick glance over Alicia's shoulder toward the other room, I kissed her neck. "Thank you," I whispered.

"So tell me about this story you're writing on Arthur," Margaret said. I set her toast and coffee and a cloth napkin on the patio table and pulled up two chairs.

I repeated what I had told her at the funeral, that my feature stories tended to be community-oriented.

"What do you mean by community-oriented?" She unfolded her napkin, rubbed out the creases, laid the napkin neatly in her lap.

I told her there were hard-working people in the community who never got the recognition they deserved. "I've always wanted to be a promoter of unsung heroes," I explained.

She raised her eyebrows above her glasses, frowning, a look of doubt tinged with bemusement. "And how would you say Arthur was an unsung hero?"

In her gray dress, with her hollow, angular face and pale skin, she looked like someone who spent all day in artificial light. Her long arms and neck, her face in the bright sunshine, gave her an unsettling force.

"He was a man with high standards. He inspired great loyalty in his friends." I was able to think of only the most general praise.

She took small bites of her toast, holding it between her bony fingers.

Joe had found a dog brush and was combing Gavin's long brindle fur front to back, muttering to himself, paying no attention to our conversation.

The coffee tasted sour. I never drank it black, but for some reason I had wanted Margaret to think that we took our coffee the same way.

"There's something you're not telling me, Mr. Hatch." She crossed her arms over her chest. "If you're expecting honest answers, you should try to be direct."

"What do you mean?" I asked, stalling.

"I loved my brother very much, but he was not the kind of man anyone would bother to write a story about. He was a do-gooder, but for himself, not anything larger. He was an ordinary man." She put the coffee cup on the ground beside her. "You're not after *Arthur's* story, are you?" she asked.

I didn't know what to say. "I'm not sure." I hesitated, defensive.

"I think you have a pretty good idea," she said. "The story you're after is Alicia."

Margaret's dark eyes zeroed in on me, as if she were after my thoughts, and I decided the best move was to confess, not to everything, but at least to reveal a small truth. Something about her demanded a confession, a kind of omniscience that seemed to say, *There's little I don't know or can't find out.*

So when she asked, "What are you really doing at this estate sale?" I broke down, first on Alicia's patio, then again and again in the weeks that would follow.

Without considering the implications, because, caught in a lie, I had to be honest about something, I said, "I'm not a reporter. I'm an obituary writer."

I told her how long I'd been on the desk and that I couldn't wait to break out, that I'd been looking for a good story to write and was frustrated until Alicia called.

"It was her idea to do the story on Arthur, not mine," I said. "I was curious, so I went along."

Had our conversation continued, I might have told her about the advancers or the ghouls or my mother's expectations. No telling how far I might have gone trying to explain, but behind me the screen door opened, and I turned around to see Alicia approaching our table.

"Hello, Margaret," she said in a flat, unfamiliar voice.

Margaret remained seated, holding her hands, palms together, in her lap.

Alicia pulled up a chair next to me, closer than I felt comfortable with. Aware of Margaret, I leaned away, resting my elbow on the chair arm.

Joe was standing up now, quietly closing the gate to the dog run, scratching Gavin's forehead through the chainlink fence. With a sidelong glance, he slunk into the house.

A cloud had drifted in front of the sun, bringing definition to Margaret's angular face. Her small mouth tensed, her eyes unblinking.

"Some of what you're selling today belonged to my mother," she said to Alicia.

Alicia looked away toward the dog run, where Gavin walked to a corner and lay down in the shade of a beech tree, resting his head on his extended paws. "I don't know why you feel that — " she began, before being interrupted by a loud crash inside the house.

We all jumped up to see what it was.

Joe Whiting stood next to the mantel over a broken Chinese vase. He was crying.

"What the hell's wrong with that guy?" one of the browsers asked, speaking to nobody in particular.

Joe was sobbing into his hands.

"No, Margaret. No. Don't be mad," he was saying.

"He just picked up that vase and threw it on the ground. Threw it! What the hell is wrong with that guy?"

Margaret took Joe's thick black glasses out of his hands, folded them, and placed them in her dress pocket. The estate sale browsers cleared a path, and with her arm around his waist, she led him back to the patio, closing the door behind her.

"He's my brother-in-law and he's limited. It was an accident," Alicia told the man who had complained. "Thank you for your help, but everything is under control now."

I went to get a dustpan and broom out of the kitchen and swept the vase into the trash. It was a lovely vase, white with orange and blue flowers and a gold band around the neck. The price was twenty-five dollars, though it must have been worth at least a couple of hundred.

"That was one of their mother's vases," Alicia said when we had both returned to the kitchen. "Joe gets incredibly tense whenever Margaret and I are in the same place. He can't stand it."

"Has it always been like that?" I asked.

"No, everything used to be fine."

"Well?" I prompted her.

"Well, Margaret used to live here. She and Arthur were roommates, I guess you could say, before Arthur and I married. She lived in the back bedroom, the pink one." Alicia sighed, as if she'd been over this too many times before. "I used to tell Arthur that bigamy was illegal in the state of Missouri, that he couldn't be married to both me and Margaret at the same time. He was never too amused by that."

"I thought you said everything used to be fine," I said.

"Fine until I insisted that she leave. She stayed on in the house for the first few months of our marriage before getting her own place nearby. I think she really believed that I was going to let her stay here." Alicia shook her head.

From the window, I watched Margaret open the passenger door of her small car and Joe lower his large frame into it. She reached across his lap to fasten the seat belt, then closed the door and walked around to the other side of the car. Without looking back, she settled into her seat, started the engine.

Joe had stopped crying and he stared straight ahead.

Margaret gave him back his glasses, which he put on with both hands, sitting up so that his head grazed the roof. She checked behind her, and as she turned the car around, putting on her blinker to make a left onto Kingshighway, Joe reached out and gripped the dashboard.

❖ 13 ❖

I HAD BEEN MEANING to move the triptych to my apartment — its walls were mostly bare, and I thought the painting
would bring some life to my living room — but every night after
work I'd go directly back to Alicia's house and every morning we'd
get out of bed too late for me to swing by Soulard before nine
o'clock. So the painting still sat in the pink room. I'd look at it
twice a day as I passed by.

On the Wednesday morning after the estate sale I noticed something that I hadn't seen before. Mostly I had been looking at the
nude's profile, the first third of the triptych — soft and ethereal,
gazing out of the portrait as if half asleep. It was what had drawn
me to the painting in the first place: the model's face, her lifelike
skin, so real I wanted to touch the canvas, but with an eerily distant
expression.

The night before, I had left a dustcloth hanging over the frame
of the last third of the painting: the model's legs from the waist
down. When I lifted the cloth off in the morning, I saw on the
nude's inner thigh a triangular birthmark the size of a quarter.

My stomach dropped.

Alicia had a triangular birthmark on her inner thigh. She called it her "dolphin fin," a blue-gray triangle near the top of her left leg. I had kissed that dolphin fin.

I waited for Alicia to get out of the shower. Even as I sat on her bed, listening to the steady rush of water, I thought, *This is a terrible idea. Everything has been perfect. Why ruin it now?*

She walked into the bedroom.

"Can I ask you a question?"

"Of course, sweetheart." She unwrapped the towel that was around her hair.

"You know that painting I wanted, the one that's in the room with your things?"

The corners of my mouth felt heavy, my skin weighted down.

"That's you in the painting, isn't it?"

Her slim body glistened, back-lit by a naked bulb in the closet. Drops of water fell from her hair, catching her waist, streaming down her calves. I tried to capture this picture permanently in my mind, thinking, *From this moment on, nothing will be the same.*

"Yes, that's me in the painting." She slipped on a pair of yellow underwear.

"So you posed nude?"

"Yes." As if it were nothing. "I used to know a painter who was quite good. He did a number of portraits of me."

"Where are the other ones?" I felt nauseated — there were more.

"Oh, I don't know. He sold most of his stuff in New York and Washington, galleries on the East Coast. I only recently had that one framed. I don't know why."

She wiggled into her jeans and slipped a shirt over her head. Lately she hadn't been wearing a bra. I loved to come up behind her in the laundry room or at the kitchen sink and slide my hands under her shirt.

"Did you pose for other painters?"

"No, just Jerry. There weren't many painters in Tucson."

She sat at her dressing table, the only piece of furniture left in the room besides the bed, and turned on the blow dryer.

Miserable, fighting not to let it show on my face, I stood up and went to Margaret's old room to finish getting dressed.

I knew how irrational I could become, all the terrible scenarios that my jealousy might conjure. In the car I turned the radio way up and sang along, trying to erase the possibility from my mind that she'd been with more than one man before me.

At work, I stopped by Research and asked one of the librarians to do a Lexis-Nexis search for any articles out of Tucson in the last ten years about a local painter whose first name was Jerry.

"I won't even ask," the librarian said, smiling. "This one might take a while."

Soon after I had sat down at my desk, Thea called.

We had spoken only twice in the past couple of weeks. The first time, I had halfheartedly offered to visit her father in the hospital, but he wasn't doing well so we postponed it. When I called back after that weekend, expecting her answering machine, she picked up, saying he had been transferred out of Intensive Care and might soon be headed home.

This time, she sounded upset.

"I tried you at home last night but couldn't reach you," she said. I could tell that she'd been crying. "I feel terrible asking you this, Gordie, but my father's having open-heart surgery this morning. I'm at the hospital."

Ritger arrived at his desk, setting down his briefcase loudly, and took off his trenchcoat and tweed cap. I hunched over the phone.

"I'm sorry," Thea said. "I thought I could handle it, but he had another heart attack. Now he's in the operating room."

"Where are you?" I asked.

"Still at the VA," she said.

"What floor?"

"I'm in the family waiting room next to Recovery. It's on the third floor."

"I'll be over as soon as I can."

I found Ritger down in the cafeteria, spooning sugar into his jumbo coffee mug.

"There's been an emergency and I'm going to need the day off," I said. I had never asked for a whole day off before, had only taken an occasional morning or afternoon, had a perfect sick record. "The person I was on the phone with is a good friend, and her father is having open-heart surgery. I'm sorry, but I have to go to the hospital."

Ritger stirred his coffee, then nodded his head.

The Veterans Hospital was surprisingly modern. I had expected to find a World War II–era building with pea-green walls and hulking equipment, but instead the place was bright and spacious, six stories high, with living plants and wide windows and young doctors striding around.

Thea was reading the *Independent* in the waiting room.

"You're here sooner than I thought." She looked surprised. Her eyes were red and swollen. "It's sweet of you to come, Gordie. I can't tell you what a wimp I am. Last night I went to bed telling myself, 'Don't call him. Please don't call. It's not fair to do this to him.'"

I leaned over and put my arms around her. "Don't be silly," I said, rubbing her back, which I couldn't help but notice was longer, less narrow than Alicia's.

Thea excused herself, taking her handbag, saying she'd be back in a minute.

I picked up the front page of the paper, concentrating on the news to keep my mind off the painter from Tucson. I hadn't been paying much attention to the world lately. Since my humiliation in the conference room I'd done little more at work than write formulaic obits, punch in, punch out. I told myself that every journalist goes through phases like this, but nevertheless it worried me.

My primary news source these days had been Alicia, who liked to call me at work to compare what she'd seen on CNN with what was coming over the AP wires. The situation in Eastern Europe had captivated her. She bought all of the news magazines as well as the *New York Times* and even the *Wall Street Journal* for its speculations on how the fall of communism might affect world markets.

The lead story today came from East Germany, where in Leipzig half a million people had gathered for peaceful demonstrations, calling for the ouster of Egon Krenz, the hard-liner who had recently replaced Erich Honecker as president. Alicia and I had talked about Honecker in the days following his resignation, and for a moment I had been tempted to tell her about the advancers — Honecker had been the last one I'd worked on before the Bette Davis fiasco — but I realized that she wasn't ready to hear the truth, and I wasn't ready to tell it.

Thea returned looking improved. She had thrown some water on her face, and much of the redness was gone from her eyes.

"All better," she said. "I just needed a little stroll through Intensive Care to cheer myself up."

She had two cans of apple juice from the vending machine. She looked pretty in her orange rayon dress with white flowers, and oddly enough, much better rested than the last time I'd seen her.

"What an amazing year it's been," she said, handing me a can. "I can't think of a better time to be working at a newspaper." She was friendly, as usual, eager for a change of subject.

"Yeah, I guess it has been pretty exciting. We've got a half-dozen reporters in Eastern Europe right now."

"Any chance they'll send you?"

It seemed such a distant consideration that I had to laugh. "I don't think so."

Ritger had told me that Marshall Holman might be the next reporter sent, possibly to Bulgaria, where a civilian coup against Zhivkov was growing more likely.

"Well, it must be great to work there," Thea said.

Soon we were joined in the waiting room by a white-haired woman, probably in her early sixties, who had the powdery look of someone much older. She sat in the chair nearest the door and opened a book of crossword puzzles.

It was past noon. Thea had said her father's surgery could last until three or four o'clock. Already I was growing restless. I had left the *Independent* so abruptly that I'd forgotten to call Alicia to tell her I wouldn't be reachable. We had fallen into a routine of talking several times a day, and now I worried that Ritger might pick up my line and say I was gone before I had a chance to tell her myself.

"I should probably check in with the office," I told Thea.

"Of course. Don't feel you have to stay, Gordie. I just panicked this morning. I'm much better now."

I sifted through my pockets for a quarter but was out of change. Thea handed me some coins.

"What got me most last night was when they shaved his chest," she said. "That's when I called you. My dad's an ape. He's got a really hairy chest, so it took them forever." She laughed, then turned serious. "He was flat on his back. It was pretty late. The way the nurses were standing over him — I've seen this picture a hundred times, but it really gave me the chills."

Out in the hallway I thought of my own father, whom I had not been allowed to see in the hospital when he was dying. It was important for Thea to be nearby, and I realized that I envied her for it. I knew there was nothing that I could have done back in 1972, a five-year-old boy in an ICU waiting room at some hospital in Chicago. But it hit me now just how much being nearby mattered.

I needed an excuse for Alicia. If she had told me she was taking the day off to see an old male friend whose father was in the hospital, I knew it would make me crazy. I'd been on the verge of crazy just this morning. I decided to tell her that I was out doing interviews — but she wasn't home.

In the waiting room, the white-haired woman had left behind her crossword puzzle. I looked to see how many squares she had filled.

"She's no Lorraine Hatch," I whispered across the room.

Thea laughed.

I sat down, and she looked at me intently. "So what went wrong that summer, Gordie?"

I was caught off guard. "What do you mean?"

"I mean, what happened to you? We were having such a nice time together, then suddenly you didn't want to see me anymore."

Not long ago, I might have confronted Thea. *You cheated on me,* I might have said, or *I thought we had an understanding that it was just the two of us,* but now I didn't know what to say. Four years was a lifetime ago. Even last month was a lifetime ago. It seemed not to matter anymore.

"I really don't remember. I think I was anxious about starting college." I wasn't looking at her, but I knew that she didn't believe me.

"It was so sudden, Gordie. I'm not resentful. It's just that I've never understood. I've always admired you, and I think I know you pretty well — except for that silence which I swear came completely out of the blue."

I didn't want to talk about this.

"I'll tell you what I think it was. This whole thing was my fault." I looked her in the eye. "I felt very attached to you that summer and I knew you were going to Brown, a thousand miles away, and I wasn't going to see you for a long time. I guess without realizing it I was trying to distance myself."

If she couldn't remember what had triggered my unhappiness, how she had casually replaced me with the garden clerk, I wasn't going to indulge her professed confusion.

"It wasn't fair of me," I said. "But I was eighteen and you never think of consequences at that age."

A silence hung in the air. The waiting room door opened and the white-haired woman returned. She picked up her book and moved to the seats closer to us.

"I should probably use the phone again." I got up. "My editor was away last time I called."

Thea shrugged. She hadn't believed a word.

It was getting past two o'clock, and still Alicia hadn't come home. Jerry the painter, the possibility that he was now living in St. Louis, entered my mind.

She'd been completely nude. God knows how many paintings she had posed for. Ten, twenty, fifty nudes on living room walls up and down the East Coast. How many people had walked into those houses and admired Alicia's body? Perhaps thousands.

And who was Jerry the painter? She said this morning he was the only one she had posed for. If she'd been a professional model, that would have been one thing — granted, I would've hated it — but posing only for Jerry made it so much worse. They must have been lovers.

I called Research.

"This is Gordon Hatch, the guy with the strange request." I tried to laugh. "Did you happen to find anything?"

"Actually, we have had some luck. We're still looking, but I've put four articles in your box from the *Tucson Register*," the librarian said. "Three are reviews of gallery openings and one is a feature. The painter's full name is Jerry Savage."

I thanked the librarian and hung up.

Jerry Savage. What kind of a name was that?

As I approached the waiting room, I could hear Thea talking about me.

"He's not my boyfriend," she was saying. "He's a friend."

I waited outside the door so as not to embarrass her.

"You must have a boyfriend, as pretty as you are," someone said.

"I've been working toward medical school. There isn't really time for boyfriends," Thea said. "I do have a cadaver named Elliot, but communication has been a definite problem." They laughed.

"This is my friend Gordie," Thea introduced me as I walked in, and the woman stood up to say hello.

"Listen, Thea, I hate to do this," I said, "but we're short-staffed today and things are getting pretty busy at the office. I think I probably ought to get back."

She seemed to force a smile. "It's okay. You were good to come."

"I'll call and see how everything went," I said. "Your dad's a soldier. He's going to be fine." I kissed Thea on the cheek. "Are you sure it's okay to go?"

"Go," she said. "Seriously. Thank you." She gave a small wave and looked away.

I was careful not to let Ritger see me as I picked up what had now grown to seven articles about Jerry Savage before leaving the office. Alicia's painter friend was fairly successful. His oils brought anywhere from five to fifteen thousand dollars. A New Yorker who had initially settled in Santa Fe, he'd found too many painters there and moved to the more workaday town of Tucson, where it was clear from the articles that he had achieved a kind of local celebrity.

Reviewers of his shows had nothing but praise. "If Francis Bacon had worked in the American desert and put his subjects not in locked rooms but out under the scorching sun," one reviewer wrote, "the result would very much resemble the work of Jerry Savage — haunting, intense, desolate."

Several reviewers remarked on what had caught my eye: his impressively real flesh tones. I read along with a perverse curiosity, expecting at any moment to come across a show called "Alicia," but was relieved to find nothing related, until the final article, dated August 2, 1985:

SAVAGE PROTÉGÉ OPENS AT THE FREEBOURNE
by Elisabeth Hall
Register Staff Writer

If imitation is the sincerest form of flattery, then Jerry Savage must be feeling quite good about himself after the first showing of his young protégé Alicia Steele at the Freebourne Gallery on Cantilever Road.

This exhibit of twenty new paintings is pure Savage.

Take "Desert I–VI," a series of landscape tableaus combining bright orange and purple hues with dusty reds and tans that made this reviewer swear Savage himself had mixed the palette. Or "Navajo: A Triptych," at 20 x 40 the largest work in the exhibit, which uses a classic Savage thematic technique: physical fragmentation of a canvas mirroring a subject's psychic and emotional disfigurement. In "Shoulders," Steele patently copies one of Savage's best-known body-as-landscape paintings, "Burden of the World." Look at the stone-gray eyes and the skin pigments and you'll surely ask yourself, "Haven't I seen this somewhere before?"

The good news is if you're going to imitate someone, it may as well be a first-rate artist, and Jerry Savage, with his national reputation, is as close to first rate as the area has to offer. Unfortunately, the paintings collected here are a pale imitation: devoid of the force, the surprise, the technical skill, the startling contradictions, and most egregiously, the originality, that this newcomer's mentor has made his reputation on.

"Alicia Steele: Mirages" runs through September 15.

Driving out to St. Charles, I became increasingly agitated. Alicia and this painter had obviously been together. It seemed odd that she had never talked about her show. I wondered whether this opening, this review even, had marked the beginning and end of her artistic career.

I considered calling Jerry Savage. At least I could look up his number and carry it around. *I have a few questions, if you don't mind. It's her jealous lover calling . . .*

I turned onto Kingshighway thinking I would bring up my discovery with Alicia, ask her the essentials, put everything out in the open. So she has an ex-boyfriend. Women have ex-boyfriends. Does it have to mean the end of the world?

But she wasn't there — and suddenly all reason abandoned me.

Two weeks ago she had given me an old tarnished key with a faded yellow sticker. For the first time I thought, *This must be Arthur's.* Of course it was his. It had to be. I'd make a new key tomorrow, throw this one in the garbage.

Inside the house, I double-locked the front door to buy myself more time in case Alicia came home. I went straight to the pink room, pulled down the shades, switched on the overhead light. I stared at the painting — head, torso, legs — and sat on the floor. Along the line of Alicia's calf was the painter's signature, SAVAGE, in sturdy capital letters, which I had never noticed before. I took a last look and did what I had wanted to do nearly a week ago: I opened the "Letters" box.

The journals were in order. Number 23, through this January, was still on top.

I wasn't the type to nose around or cross the boundary into people's private lives, even those closest to me, but now I was furious. Four notebooks from the top, I found what I was looking for:

JOURNAL

NO. 19

JUNE 1985–APRIL 1986

I flipped to August 2, the day of her art show opening, and began reading back in time.

14

August 2

I'm through with Jerry. Tonight. Tomorrow. Soon.

This morning at the breakfast table when he read that review, I knew I had to leave. He'll let me. That's the good thing. There's nothing worse than a clinger. He'll miss having someone around to bitch to, that's for sure, about the Philistine buyers, how he's misunderstood, how he suffers for going it alone. He'll miss the sex that he thinks he's good at and someone other than himself to blame, because the light's not right in the gallery, the day slips by too fast, don't shower so long we're low on water. Where did you put my Naples red? You know my reds are off limits.

The door will be open. I'll be free to go. He doesn't care and he never did. Boo hoo.

I don't know what happened, how I ever landed here. Why do I always catch men on the downslope? A climber would be nice for a change. Jerry was going down. Whatever Elisabeth Hall, Miss Small-Time High-Culture America, says, he's a washed-up has-been. Didn't know it then, but I know it now. I fell for his paintings, not him. That was it. All the life that those paintings promised was gone in the day-to-day. He must have painted the soul right out of himself. Splatter! Splat! Now there's nothing.

This morning he looks up from his cereal. Grape Nuts three times a day. It's all he eats. He says to me, "Jeez. You're not going to like this." I reach for the newspaper and he's sort of holding it against his chest, with a stupid little frown, a cock of the head, a look on his face: I'm-only-trying-to-protect-you.

"They reviewed my show?" I ask.

And this is what I see: his face (what you can make of it behind the Castro beard) has only a thin film of sympathy. It isn't even sympathy. It's the show of sympathy. Beneath it, brimming from head to toe, is a sick satisfaction.

"Maybe we should throw this away," he says.

He's too comfortable, that's the problem. People around here love him because there's nobody else. He's the only thing going. That's why he's married to Tucson. He had no competition before I came around.

It wasn't until this morning that I realized it was a competition. Had been from the first canvas he gave me. Amazing after more than a year that I had no idea. Now all those green-eyed looks come back to me — "Sneer, Scoff, Snicker, Sneeze," montage by Jerry Savage.

I couldn't help myself; I had to read more, go even further into the past.

October 16, 1982

Why is it I'm only shy around men my age?

Kyle, Rodeo Kyle, comes into the store and I lean back on the stairs, a blushing wallflower.

I never much went for the rodeo boys growing up. In Dallas there were just too many of them — we'd tease them behind their tight Wranglers — but out here I see I must have had a secret fondness all along for the saddle riders of Weatherford.

He strides in, not cocky, and picks up his mail every day between 1:30 and 2, lays his letters on the counter. Why? So I can see who they're from: just bill collectors. Is that it? He goes around to the coolers for a bottle of cream soda. Every day, a cream soda. He puts down his money without a word, then he's gone.

I turned the page, disbelieving. Had I not known about Jerry Savage or been able to recognize Alicia's handwriting, I would have sworn that these were written by a different person. This was the voice of an experienced woman, someone who had been around.

Her entries were sporadic. Sometimes a week or two would pass, sometimes a day; some entries would be a line long — "Saw a six-foot bull snake slither out of the shed" or "Thinking about the city again"; some entries would go on for pages. Enough was enough, but one word caught my eye.

> Sex with Kyle is the best ever.
> Is it cliché that he's a rodeo cowboy? Somehow too staged? Where does he get that giddyup at the end of a working day? He says just looking at me. We fit like (name your simile).

I closed the notebook. Her life was at the extension of my arm. For a price, a terrible price that I sensed I was already beginning to pay, I could know exactly who she was.

At eight o'clock Alicia came home with a bag of groceries.

I had calmed myself down, pacing about, cleaning the kitchen and sweeping dust out of corners where the furniture had been.

"I don't know why I went to the grocery store," she said. "We're not going to be here for a couple of days."

"What do you mean?"

"The painters are coming tomorrow. We'll have to go to your place."

Alicia had never been to my apartment. I'd been back myself only a couple of times in the past two weeks.

"For how long? You know it's really small."

"They said it won't be more than two days, plus another to air the place out." She put the groceries on the counter: milk, coffee, essentials. "They're sending a big team."

We hadn't talked much about Alicia's future plans. She knew she wanted to put the house on the market, which had pleased me considerably — it would be her final act of looking past Arthur.

But now Arthur was only one of who knew how many men Alicia was looking past. Selling the house seemed less urgent, even less sensible now.

"I saw the realtor today and took Arthur's clothes to Goodwill," she said. "It was such a relief giving them away. You know what happens to widows who keep their husbands' clothing in the closet? They keep going back in there looking for memories. Movie stubs in blazer pockets. Little notes and lost dollar bills.

"I'm not going to be one of those widows," she said. "It's terrible what they do to themselves. And they can't help it — standing in closets and closing their eyes, breathing the scent on the collars of those shirts. Every scent a memory of something."

I thought of Margaret, imagined how upset she would be if she found out about Arthur's clothes.

Alicia put the milk in the refrigerator.

"I can't wait to be finished with all these errands," she said. "It's time to get focused."

I couldn't think of a thing to say.

"I also got the papers." She brightened. "The Berlin Wall is coming down by the weekend. Mark my words."

I decided now wasn't the time to confront her about Jerry. I'd head back to my apartment to clean up before she came over a few hours later.

"What should we do about dinner?" I asked finally.

"I've already eaten."

The heat rose in me again as I thought, *With whom?*

"You have?"

"I was hungry." She shrugged.

I drew a rough map from St. Charles to my apartment in Soulard for her and said I'd see her at ten.

"Goodbye, sweetheart." She kissed me.

On the road to St. Louis, *Sex with Kyle is the best ever* darted around my brain. Black ink in Alicia's own hand.

I pulled off I-70 to Highway 40 and found an all-night, all-everything store. I bought a dozen votive candles, a bar of oatmeal soap, a tape of Patsy Cline's greatest hits, two bottles of fifteen-dollar French wine, even a bouquet of cut flowers, still reasonably fresh.

Tonight I would make those journals obsolete. I would be the best ever, *the only one,* driving Kyle and Jerry Savage and Arthur Whiting and who cared who else out of her memory for good.

Three messages were on the answering machine. The first was from Thea.

"Thanks again for coming this morning, Gordie. My dad came out of the operation fine. He didn't get to Recovery until an hour ago, so I would have taken your whole day." She sounded run-down. "They found a couple of blockages that hadn't shown up on the angiogram, but he's out of surgery and babbling nonsense, so everything's A-okay."

She'd be spending the night in the hospital. Her father, she guessed, wouldn't be out for another five or six days.

My mother's was the next. Since my visit home, I had rarely been returning her calls, which made her hysterical. But here she sounded relaxed, so much so, I thought, that with Alicia's arrival still an hour away, I'd call her.

"You're a sweetie pie, Gordie," she said. The old Zenith was on in the background. A studio laugh track. She never used to watch television at this hour. "Thea told me you spent the whole day with her. That was extremely decent. I can promise you it's something she'll never forget."

I sensed her stretching the phone over to the television as she turned the sound down. "I remember every person who came to visit when your father was dying. Every single one."

It had been so long since we'd had a normal conversation that I almost didn't know what to say. "When did you talk to Thea?" I asked.

"About an hour ago."

"Only family was allowed in the recovery room. I haven't heard about the operation."

"I don't think it was particularly successful," she said. "When they went in, they found much more damage than they'd expected."

I heard the flick of a lighter, her sharp inhale. I pictured her licking her lips, the way she did when she took a cigarette from her mouth to talk.

"They usually hope for ten years after a bypass, but the doctors have been reticent. Thea sounds okay, but you know how bottled up she is. Suffer in silence."

I opened some windows to air out the apartment, took a broom from the hall closet, and began sweeping. Talking to my mother was taking my mind off Alicia's secrets.

"I tried to get the day off, but there's a bug going around and I'm all that's left," she said. "Dean Cantor wouldn't let me go. I practically run the place and he wouldn't let me go."

"So you almost came here?"

"Oh yes," she said. "I would have been there tonight."

I looked at the bottles of wine, the flowers lying on the kitchen counter, and considered what a disaster that might have been. "Well, I should probably go," I said. "I'm out with the police reporters tonight. We've had a rash of payback killings."

"Be careful," my mother said.

I got off the phone with a sinking feeling, a passing sadness. Why lie? She hadn't forced me this time. Not a single question about work. This phone call had been different; I'd seen how it could be with my mother, someday, when her expectations were met.

The last message was from Margaret.

"This is Margaret Whiting. I wanted to follow up on our conversation from last weekend." The line had the muffled echo of long distance or a cordless phone. "If you could call me tomorrow I would be grateful."

She left both her home and work numbers. I wondered what kind of work she did. I figured maybe she taught elementary school: strict, orderly, old-fashioned.

I had expected, even on the answering machine message, some kind of apology or explanation for Joe's outburst, but Margaret, I would see, was unapologetic, believing, when it came down to it, that discussion ends with the act.

I slid the bottles of wine into the freezer. Without a vase for the flowers, I put what was left of my Maxwell House into a plastic bag and the flowers in the coffee can, and set the arrangement on the living room chest, where it looked nice and rustic.

I put the Patsy Cline tape in the cassette player and lit the dozen votives, which I placed around the living room, on my bedside table and bureau, turning off all the lights. I took a long shower with the oatmeal soap, shaved my face smooth, dressed in a pair of comfortable pants and my favorite threadbare button-down shirt, and waited for Alicia to buzz the intercom.

By the time she arrived, more than an hour late, I'd had three glasses of wine, the votives were getting down to their tins, and Patsy Cline was singing "I Fall to Pieces" a second time around.

"This place isn't so small." She turned on the overhead light, then poked her head into my bedroom, where she dropped her bag.

"How about some wine?" I asked, filling a glass.

"No, I'm fine. I'm too tired to drink."

"Are you sure? It'll help you sleep."

"Maybe a couple of aspirin." She dropped to the couch. "Do you have some juice or something?"

I brought her a glass of orange juice and some Tylenol and sat next to her, reaching my arm across the top of the couch. I combed the curls back off her forehead with my fingers, wiped the perspiration through her hair. Kissing her temple I noticed the brown roots that were coming in. I never used to like dyed hair, in the same way that I couldn't stand makeup or chewing gum or high-heeled shoes, but on Alicia brown roots looked sexy — the woman in transition again, changing her look especially for me.

"What time is it?"

I gestured at the kitchen clock, which read a quarter to eleven.

"I'm going to take a shower." She sat up. "Do you have cable? I don't want to miss the news."

"I only have regular TV."

"Huh." She went to the bedroom and undressed. I turned off the Patsy Cline tape, blew out the votives, poured the glass of wine in the sink.

Alicia returned, freshly scrubbed, in a huge black and gray Colorado football T-shirt that fell nearly to her knees.

My heart sank. A football player, some enormous hulking brute, had given this to her.

"What's that box?" she asked now, pointing to the scanner, which sat on top of the television. I hadn't turned it on in weeks.

"A police radio."

"Why do you have it?"

"To know what's happening in the streets. I listen to it all the time."

I turned it on, flipping between stations. "Any good reporter should have one of these," I boasted.

"But you're an investigative reporter."

I pressed up behind her, sliding my hands under her shirt. "I like to keep a feel for the city," I said, squeezing her shoulders. "If something really good comes over, I'll go out to the crime scene."

"You go to crime scenes?" She turned around, suddenly interested. "I've always wondered what that would be like."

The dispatcher on Channel 3 was sending two cars to break up a party in South Grand.

"I go all the time," I said.

"Let's go, then," she said, and she meant *right now*. "I just need to put on some jeans."

She came back from the bedroom in her jeans with the football shirt untucked, and turned up the volume on the scanner. I tried telling her that nothing was happening, it wasn't a good night for crime scenes, praying all along, *Please, let's not have a shooting.* Each time I attempted to distract her, she raised her hand to indicate, *Not now, I'm trying to listen.*

The police had broken up the party without incident; the dispatchers were going through their neighborhood checks. After a while, she began to look tired again. It was well past midnight, and I had work in the morning.

"I'll tell you what," I said. "How about you come by the office tomorrow night after work and I'll show you around the newspaper. We can do the crime scene another night."

She didn't argue, and later I watched her beneath the Fred Astaire poster, her head on my pillow, surrounded by my clothes and my photographs.

I climbed into bed and curled my body behind hers, kissing the ridge of her shoulder, breathing in the sweet scent of oatmeal soap.

15

AT WORK Thursday morning there was a note on my desk saying that Ritger had called and he wouldn't be in for the rest of the week. The number he left, in case of emergency, was not his home telephone, so I looked it up in the crisscross directory: Sandy Hill Rehabilitation Center.

His jaw again.

This wouldn't be the first time that he'd gone back for a major treatment. He'd been back twice before, each time returning to work in a foul humor. Once he'd slept on it badly and the jaw had to be realigned; the other time they'd actually rebroken it, putting him on a painkiller that made veins rise around his forehead and neck.

But something countered my good mood that morning. On the way back from the cafeteria I'd noticed that the painting in the lobby — the reproduction of Remington's *Pony Express,* the first sight to greet me each day as the doors opened to the newsroom — had taken on new meaning. Beneath the flaring nostrils of the horse and its eager rider was the sweeping orange cursive of Bobby Campanis.

I could look nowhere, it seemed, without facing Alicia's past.

Around lunchtime, Margaret called from what sounded like a busy restaurant.

"Shall we pick up where we left off?" she asked.

I couldn't remember just where we had left off, only that she had begun to draw the truth out of me before Alicia interrupted us.

"You were telling me that you're an obituary writer," she said. "I appreciated your honesty, so I thought I'd return the favor."

I heard a door slide shut, drowning out the noise of the busy restaurant.

"I know you're not writing a story about my brother, Mr. Hatch — we've been over that — and I won't pry into your motivations. But I thought you'd be interested in knowing a bit about Alicia."

"Anything you'd like to tell me, I'm happy to hear," I said.

"The first time I met her was at the wedding," Margaret began. "Their courtship was extremely brief."

She said the wedding took place down in the Ozarks, where the Whitings owned a cabin on Table Rock Lake, thirty miles from the Arkansas border. The cabin, which had been in the family since 1939, sat at the tip of a long point on twenty-five acres of open field. Arthur's father liked to fish there. His mother raised wolfhounds.

"We'd have the puppies whelped by June," Margaret said. "By August they'd all be in good homes."

She knew exactly how many dogs her family had brought into the world: sixty-eight, in fifteen litters. She had kept close track of them, counting dozens of prize winners in the family pedigree.

When both their mother and father died unexpectedly within a year of each other, leaving Margaret, the oldest and still in high school, in the role of surrogate parent, Arthur became obsessed with carrying on the tradition — first as a handler, then as a trainer, breeder, and judge. He never owned fewer than a dozen wolfhounds at a time, all of them show quality.

"Dogs were the passion of his life," Margaret said.

It was natural, then, that he would give Alicia a puppy as a wedding gift.

"Who was at the wedding?"

"That was a curious thing. She didn't have anyone there, not even her parents. I believe they live in Texas."

"Her parents? Aren't they dead?"

"They're not dead," she said. "At least they weren't three years ago. Alicia tells lies of convenience."

I thought if anyone had been untruthful thus far in my short time with Alicia, it had been me.

"Would you like to know how they met?"

"Sure," I said hesitantly.

"Alicia came into the bank for a ten-thousand-dollar loan, and he fell for her instantly." She laughed bitterly, the kind of laugh that seemed on the edge of tears. "She never did pay the loan back. Arthur did."

I was fidgeting with the phone cord, twisting and untwisting it around my finger.

"And something else," she continued. "Alicia didn't look at all like she does now."

According to Margaret, in the fall of 1986 Alicia had a strung-out look. Her skin was pale and drawn, her hair spiked, rust red. She couldn't have weighed more than a hundred pounds.

"Even in her wedding dress she looked like a stray," Margaret said.

"I have a hard time believing she ever looked like that," I said.

"Perhaps I should send you a photograph. I know how implausible it must seem."

I paused. "Okay."

"The physical change was almost immediate," she said. "When I saw them that spring, her color was more natural and she had gained weight. By fall, she looked like she does today."

Alicia found work with a local veterinarian, took up dog grooming, trained to be a handler. She began dressing like the ladies in the dog club and became increasingly obsessed with making her puppy a champion.

"She's utterly transient," Margaret said. The judgment in her voice put me on the defensive. "Because she had no life of her own, she moved into Arthur's and completely took over."

I didn't wish to hear any more. I knew if Margaret carried on much further I might say something I'd regret, so I told her that I ought to be getting back to work, perhaps we'd be in touch. But before I hung up I couldn't resist trying to learn more about their falling-out.

"At the estate sale, Alicia told me that you used to live in her house," I said.

"It's not her house, it's Arthur's," Margaret shot back. "He bought it."

"But you used to live there, right?"

"I had been looking to settle back down in St. Louis, so I moved in with my brother temporarily. That was 1982. Headquarters had moved me to Ohio for a couple of years, to open a new branch office."

Margaret had struck me as anything but the corporate type. I'd been guessing that she was a schoolteacher.

"Where do you work?"

"Ralston Purina," she said. Purina headquarters was in St. Louis, and now it made sense.

"So you lived at the house on Dalecarlia for what, four years?" I asked.

"It was only meant to be a few months, as I said, but as so often happens, the months turned into years. The best four years in my memory, if you want to know the truth. Arthur and I had very few people in our lives, so we were a great comfort to each other."

"And then Alicia came along?"

"That's right," Margaret said. "And getting rid of me was her first order of business."

"So you moved out when she moved in?"

"I think everything would have been fine. I didn't plan to stay there forever, but she gave Arthur an ultimatum. 'It's me or your sister,' she said, and for whatever reason — perhaps because he was inexperienced with women and thought he had fallen in love — he didn't even try to stand up to her." Margaret was silent. I could hear the din of the restaurant she was calling from in the background. "From then on, it was never the same."

I didn't know how to respond.

"So, where can I send the wedding picture?" she asked.

I gave her my address at the office, and said goodbye.

The Berlin Wall opened at the stroke of midnight German time, five P.M. U.S. Central, that same day, Thursday, November 7. I had finished six obituaries and moved them to the copy desk, anticipating that Alicia would phone and want to talk about this historic moment.

Her call came at one minute after five. "Are you watching?"

"Why did I know it was you?" I leaned back in my chair, resting my feet on an open file drawer.

"It's incredible, isn't it? Look at all those people!"

The nearest television was halfway across the newsroom, suspended over the metro cluster. A small crowd stood under it watching.

"This is the beginning of the end, you know. They're going to take down the wall and the two Germanys will come together and communism's going to be just a word for the history books," she said. "No more lies and propaganda. That dream is about to end."

I wasn't sure what Alicia had been reading, but lately when we talked about world events, or rather, when she expounded on the news of the moment, I felt as if I were listening to a television commentator. As much as her interest pleased me, she was beginning to sound remote.

"So, when are you coming down?" I asked.

She seemed irritated by my attempt to change the subject, but said she wouldn't be too long. She wanted to watch the rest of the commentary, wait for the crowd on the East Berlin side to thin.

After the six-thirty meeting I ate a quick dinner in the cafeteria, watching the nightly news with a couple of press operators who were soon to begin their shift.

I introduced myself to the one with "Foreman" stitched on the chest of his blue jumpsuit. "We've got a new reporter coming in tonight," I said, sounding official. "She's about to head off for Eastern Europe and I wondered if I could walk her through the pressroom when the first edition starts rolling."

The foreman went on for a while about union rules — the pressroom was generally off limits to the rest of the building — but in the end he handed me two pairs of yellow foam earplugs.

"You'll need these," he said. "It's worse than a Who concert down there."

The research library was on my way back to the newsroom, so I stopped off.

"I'm trying to find somebody in Texas named Steele," I explained to the nightside librarian, who was eating dinner while watching CNN. "If there is a listing, it would be outside of Dallas, in a town called Weatherford."

The librarian pointed with a piece of garlic bread to an overstuffed shelf. "Phone books," he said, his mouth full.

Of the thirty-two Steeles in the greater Dallas–Fort Worth area, only one was listed in Weatherford: Jacqueline. I took down the number and folded it into my wallet, pleased to think that Alicia had been telling me the truth — her parents, it appeared, were both dead. Jacqueline Steele was probably an aunt.

By the time Alicia called from the security desk, the only people left in the newsroom were the night city editor, a handful of copy editors, a general assignment reporter who was watching the wires for updates, and Jessie Tennant.

I hadn't seen Jessie Tennant in a month. I'd been coming in at ten, never leaving past six. She hadn't responded after my brief thank-you note. Now, on my way to the elevators, I watched her, posture-perfect over her keyboard, a broad-brimmed hat resting at her elbow.

"Your elevator talks," Alicia said, stepping out into the lobby as the doors closed behind her.

"You've never heard a talking elevator?" I led her by the hand to the *Pony Express* mural. "You've probably seen something like this before, though."

She was looking toward the newsroom.

"Recognize the signature?" I asked, pointing to the sweeping "Bobby Campanis" in the lower right-hand corner.

Alicia's mind was elsewhere. "Oh." She smiled. "That's funny."

We stopped at the wire machines and Alicia scrolled through the news.

"It's fascinating, all the East Germans camping out on the Kurfürstendamm," she said. "Thousands of them, waiting all night for the fancy West Berlin shops to open. They're dying to see prosperity up close."

St. John's office was unlocked, so we went inside for his view of the city.

It was a clear night. Looking east from his floor-to-ceiling window we could see the white lights around the cupola of the old courthouse, the red warning light at the top of the Gateway Arch, the small lit squares of hotel rooms rising over the river, the approaching yellow light of a train coming west out of Illinois.

"So this is your office?" Alicia asked. She was running her hand along the edge of St. John's polished mahogany desk.

"No, actually, it's my editor's office."

"It's nice," she said. "Where's yours?"

Every office had a nameplate, so I couldn't exactly lie. But she knew I was a young reporter, and young reporters have to start somewhere. She'd understand.

"I'm across the way," I said.

I told her about the layout of the *Independent* newsroom, how it was modeled after the *Washington Post*. All the offices were made of glass so editors and reporters could each see what the others were doing.

"It's what journalism is all about," I said. "No secrets. Everything comes out into the open."

We walked along the east wall and I showed her National and Business, Layout and Editorial, pointing out desks of reporters and columnists whose bylines she would recognize.

She looked at me thoughtfully, admiration in her eyes. She wanted to know everything. I felt like putting my arm around her as if to say, *All this is mine.*

In the middle of the metro area, we stopped at Jessie Tennant's desk.

"This is my friend Alicia," I said.

Jessie Tennant smiled and shook Alicia's hand, then turned to me with a look of concern.

"How have you been?" she asked.

And before she could say *I haven't seen you in a while* or *I've been worried about you,* I interrupted her.

"Oh, great, fine," I said, as if the Bette Davis disaster had never happened. "Business as usual. You know how it is."

She glanced at Alicia, understanding that I was trying to make an impression.

"I've read your columns," Alicia told her. "They're very power-ful. Especially the human interest stories. I have to tell you, I wept when I read your pieces about Michael Moseby." Back in Septem-ber, a death-row inmate had been released when another man, on death row in a different state, confessed to the killing for which Moseby had gone to prison. Jessie Tennant had written a series of columns about Moseby's family and their fifteen-year fight to clear his name. "I can think of nothing more terrible than being accused of a murder you didn't commit," Alicia said.

Jessie Tennant nodded her head.

As we were leaving, she touched Alicia's arm. "Gordon has a bright future in this business," she said. "He's got integrity, which means the path will always be brambled. But I think he'll be one of the really good ones."

It was a typically moral Jessie Tennant remark, and I loved it.

It was ten-thirty already, the usual start time for the first edition. I removed the earplugs from my pocket, handing a pair to Alicia. We took the back stairs down to the pressroom, in the basement of the *Independent* building.

Our timing was perfect.

Rounding the last flight of steps, we could hear the rumble of the presses starting up. By the time we reached the entrance, the great metal rollers were screaming. At the black swinging doors, marked AUTHORIZED on one side and PERSONNEL on the other in bold red letters, Alicia and I put in our earplugs.

The expression on her face was pure happiness. She mouthed the word "ready."

I tried to look indifferent, as if I did this all the time. With the earplugs in, I could hear nothing but my own pulse, the blood coursing through my veins.

Inside the pressroom, the air was humid, the smell choking, like wet tar on a hot day. We walked carefully over the stamped-metal floor between two long rows of gigantic sky-blue presses. The first edition flew along the rollers in one long sheet, the black ink on white paper a gray blur. Under our feet, the floor trembled. The pressmen, in their smudged navy blue uniforms, strolled casually through the aisles and around the great machines, accustomed to their power.

Walking amidst the deafening noise, able to hear nothing more than a steady hum, the power was physical, doubly intense. My ribs lifted in my chest; my heart was racing. At the end of the aisle I spotted the foreman from the cafeteria coming down a winding staircase with a stack of newspapers. I waved and he came over, handing me a first edition, still warm.

The banner headline, above a fifty-seven-pica photograph of the first East Berliners crossing into the West, read: FREEDOM!

Back in the newsroom, we took out our earplugs.

"So, show me your office," she said.

I walked her back to Obituaries, where the lead-removing fan clattered noisily above my desk.

"It's not really an office," I said.

She looked around, clearly disappointed. She reached up to touch the black-ribbed tubing. "What's this?" she asked.

"It's part of a renovation," I said.

"This is where you *work?*"

I hesitated. "Not always."

"Look where they've put you, Gordie." She turned to survey the newsroom. "This isn't right."

I was going to tell her that there's a hierarchy to everything, you have to start somewhere, everyone pays his dues.

"You should be in one of those big offices over there," she said, the color rising in her face. "This is crazy. Who do they think you are?"

"It's not so important where my desk is," I tried to say, startled by her sudden anger.

"Of course it is. You can't let people step on you like this. They'll crush you."

She slammed her hand on my desk and walked away.

I followed her across the newsroom into the lobby, where we waited in silence for the elevator to arrive.

"You're right," I said finally, to cool her down. "I'll talk with somebody about it in the morning."

❖ 16 ❖

ON MONDAY MORNING, signs of Ritger's return littered his desk: a half-eaten pen, his monogrammed handkerchief, a rubber ball he liked to squeeze.

When I signed on to the computer, he had sent me a message. "We had to run a correction," it read. "You fucked up somebody's age."

I opened the morning paper to page A2:

> April Wellstone died last Thursday, November 7. She was 76. In all Sunday editions of the obituary page, her age was listed incorrectly as 68.

It was a common problem, one that had happened before, and not just to me but to Ritger as well. A woman dies who has been lying about her age; her sister says nothing about it when she calls in the obituary. A day or so later, a nurse or an old friend, someone who knows the woman's actual age, calls up the desk asking for a correction.

Ritger's policy had always been, "So it goes." If the family's going to bend the truth, the newspaper shouldn't be held responsible for it. We had never run a correction before in such a case as this.

"Her sister told me sixty-eight," I wrote him back. "She lied, so why the correction?"

He responded immediately. "You know perfectly well why the correction," his message read. "It's called journalistic accuracy."

I didn't dwell on Ritger. A month before, his message would have been devastating — I would have been sick with worry — but for some reason it didn't bother me now.

I decided to try Jacqueline Steele's number, waiting three long rings before a soft-spoken woman answered the phone.

"Is this Mrs. Jacqueline Steele?"

"Yes it is."

"I'm a reporter doing a feature story on Alicia Steele," I said. "I've done a number of interviews with her friends and colleagues and am eager to speak with family. Are you related to Alicia Steele?"

There was a long silence, the sound of a lawnmower off in the distance. I hadn't prepared any specific questions. I was surprised to have gotten through.

"She's my daughter," the woman said.

"Your daughter?"

"What's she done?" she asked.

"Nothing." Stunned, I managed to add, "I'm just doing a feature on her painting."

"I didn't know about her painting." Mrs. Steele coughed.

"Well, I'll be in Texas on Wednesday on another story," I said. "Perhaps I can swing by your house on my way through Dallas."

I didn't know what I was committing myself to — the words had just come out. I had work on Wednesday. There wouldn't be time to arrange for vacation. I'd have to call in sick or make something up. My father had dropped everything and left on a whim for Dallas. Why shouldn't I?

"Why do you need to talk to me?" she asked.

I didn't have an answer. "I just need to." I sounded impatient.

There was a long pause. "I haven't seen Alicia in fifteen years. I'm sorry," Mrs. Steele said. "I just can't." She fumbled the phone and hung up.

I found the travel agent in the Yellow Pages with the biggest ad and bought a round-trip ticket to Dallas leaving Wednesday morning, returning the same day. It cost a week's salary on such short notice, and there was no guarantee that Mrs. Steele would even be there, much less willing to talk. I didn't know what had gotten into me. I was going on journalistic instinct.

My mother called as I was studying a map of Dallas and the outlying suburbs, drawing up a rough itinerary.

"So what do you want for your birthday?" In the chaos of my current situation, I had forgotten that my birthday was that Thursday.

Her call was serendipitous, because I was already living paycheck to paycheck and couldn't afford the ticket I had just bought. "It's funny you should mention it," I said.

I told her about the trip to Dallas, thought about saying it was for a story that I'd been working on, but she wouldn't have understood why I'd need the money.

They're not paying for you to go? she'd have said. *If they can't afford you now, how do they expect to afford you when you're in demand?*

I told her that I was going to Dallas not on assignment but for something else, something personal. On the verge of my first breakthrough, I'd decided to go for the day, to be where my father was at the same moment in his career.

"It's a pilgrimage," I said.

The only problem, I explained, was how to afford it. I'd already bought the ticket — impulsively, I had to admit — but this was important to me. It was worth any sacrifice.

"For my birthday all I want is a few dollars to help pay the fare," I said. "Everything's been arranged."

My mother's voice got quiet. "I don't know if I like the idea. What are you going to do there?"

I told her I'd go to the Book Depository and the area around

Dealey Plaza, check out my father's old office on Commerce Street, drive by the house where he lived, maybe ask the owners if I could come inside and take a look. I said I might call a few of his old friends — Bob Strampe, Dave Vance, Skip Kaler — beat reporters from the local press whose names I knew from my mother's stories. But mostly I wanted to be in the place where he had been.

"I've never been there," I said. "I want to go."

She let out a cough. "Bob Strampe died in 1981, and I'd be surprised if the others are still there. There's an office complex where the house used to be. Dallas grew too fast."

She said it was a sweet idea and she understood why I would want to go, but with so little left to connect my father's time with the present day, I might find the trip a disappointment.

"It's best to leave Dallas in the imagination," she said.

When I had convinced her that there was no talking me out of it, that I had already made my decision, that even if I changed my mind the ticket was nonrefundable, she turned to the upcoming weekend.

"I hope you'll be back in time," she said.

"It's a one-day trip. I have to get back to finish my story anyway."

"I'll send you the money," she said. "But I'm still coming to see you."

Just as my birthday had slipped my mind, so had the news of my mother's visit. I vaguely remembered a brief conversation from a couple of weeks ago. The timing could not have been worse, but there was nothing to do for it now.

When I came back from lunch, Ritger's chair was pushed in. I signed on to the computer, expecting some kind of message from him, but there was nothing, only an All News announcement saying that the lead removal program was in its final stages; the environment would be clear of toxins by the end of the month.

I checked the mail, and at the bottom of the pile was a number 10 envelope from Margaret Whiting.

"As you requested . . . ," she had written on a note, leaving a daytime and evening telephone number and a number for the Ralston Purina marketing department in Cleveland, where she would be on business until the end of the week. Inside were three color photographs — three-by-fives, unprofessional, and taken from a less than ideal distance — one of the bride and groom, the bride and groom with Margaret and Joe, and Alicia standing alone in front of the lake.

What Margaret had said was true. Alicia looked completely different. Her cheeks were sunken and she had a startled look in her eyes. Her hair, dyed red, lay limp about her shoulders, her bangs sticking up. She was thin as kindling.

In the solo shot, out on the point of Table Rock Lake, Alicia's arms hung loosely at her sides. Her head looked like a weight atop her small neck.

I called Margaret at the business number in Ohio.

She answered immediately.

"Are you busy?" I asked.

"I'm between meetings," she said.

"I got your letter. Thank you." It was strange to say thank you, considering what I held in my hands. But these were only pictures, I told myself. A person in a picture is not a person at all. I would see Alicia soon, and this pale woman from three years ago, this "stray," as Margaret had called her, would be the furthest thing from my mind.

"I'm sending them back." I decided then and there, and slid the pictures into a fresh envelope, sealing it.

"Were you surprised?" Margaret asked.

"No, not particularly." I was beginning to wish I hadn't called.

"You see what I mean? She looked totally different."

The way Alicia looked was not something I wanted to discuss

with Margaret. Anything else was fine — Arthur, Joe, her parents, even her feelings about the marriage, the wedding, the past — but how Alicia looked, her physical appearance, that made me uncomfortable.

"Well? She does look entirely different now, doesn't she?" Margaret pressed.

"Alicia's mother is still alive," I burst out, trying to change the subject. It was a careless slip, I would later recall, playing it over in my mind.

"Really?"

Recklessly, I said, "She lives in a place called Weatherford. She hasn't seen her daughter in fifteen years."

"My goodness." Margaret drew out the words.

I did the math for the first time. Alicia had left home at seventeen.

"Where is Alicia planning to go now?"

"You mean where is she moving to?"

"Yes. Where is she moving to?"

"I don't know. I haven't seen her in a while," I lied.

"Didn't she sell most of her possessions at the estate sale?" Margaret asked.

"I think you're right, she did." I hesitated.

"So everything is sold, the house is empty, and she has no idea where she's moving to?"

"Last I heard she's staying in the area."

Margaret cleared her throat. Even on the phone, I could sense her anger rising.

"I think I understand why she would want to get on with her life," I offered cautiously. "She's so young, and when something like that happens, in a way it's best to start over."

"You're wrong about her," Margaret said. "It's okay to set the past aside for a time, but you can't discard it. You can't just pick up, clean the slate, and become someone else." I heard somebody whispering in the background. "I'll just be another minute," Margaret told the person, then got back on the phone. "Maybe I neglected to tell you about my brother's will."

"He had a will?" It seemed unusual that anyone would have a will at forty-three, without any children.

"We wrote up our wills while we were living at the house on Dalecarlia, before Alicia," Margaret explained. "Our family has a terrible history of heart disease. Both of our parents had heart attacks, and my father died of one, so we did it just to be sure.

"It had nothing to do with money," she said after a moment. "Neither of us had much anyway. The wills were just part of our bond, a way of ensuring that each of our lives mattered and would continue to matter if something were to happen. We were especially concerned about Joe's livelihood if one of us were gone."

I sensed where this story was heading. "So when Arthur married Alicia, he changed his will."

"Of course. Alicia had complete control over him almost immediately, and he signed everything over to her. The dogs, his share of the Winfield farm, the house, all of its contents. And now she's just getting rid of it all, piece by piece, as fast as she can."

Out of the corner of my eye, I saw Ritger making his way toward the desk. His jaw was wired shut. His face was deep vermilion. I got off the phone quickly.

He took a reporter's notebook from the inside pocket of his tailored suit and, standing over me, scratched out a message, the pen nearly ripping the paper as he wrote.

The company does not pay for your personal business!

"What do you mean?" I asked.

A call to Texas at 11:30 A.M. None of our stiffs has relatives there. I checked the log.

I didn't know what to say. I wasn't aware of a company policy regarding long-distance calls. Reporters were free to make them, I assumed, so long as it was for a story. Mine could have been for a story.

How had he found out, I wondered. He reached over and hit the redial button.

"Who ish dish?" he spat through his metalwork, the veins in his neck standing out like snakes.

"What shitty ish dish?" he asked.

Slamming down the phone, he wrote me a note:

Fucking Ohio!

Someone other than Margaret had obviously picked up, and now I was in trouble. Ritger stormed away.

I did my best to look busy for the rest of the afternoon. I scraped together the day's obituaries, ran around the newsroom with a determined look, appearing as though routine tasks were thrilling. During the six-thirty meeting, I cleaned up some files that I hadn't touched in months, dusted around the desk, replenished our stock of dummy sheets, legal paper, notebooks, and pens. After the meeting was over and the newsroom had begun to empty of daysiders, I signed on to the computer one last time.

"I've spoken with Dick," read a message from St. John. "Keep this up and your job is more than on the line."

It was seven, now dark, when I arrived home. The painters had finished Alicia's house over the weekend, and she had moved back to St. Charles in the morning. We had decided for the first time since getting together three weeks ago to spend a night on our own. After four days in my cramped apartment we had both become tense.

It felt strange eating dinner alone. I pictured Alicia in the photograph, sunken and pale, thought of what Margaret had said about the will and how Alicia was thoughtlessly discarding the past, and I realized how much easier life had been before I'd cared about knowing the truth.

Already I missed her. I wanted to call, but we'd agreed that morning that I'd see her tomorrow. By nine o'clock, though, I couldn't stand the thought of sleeping alone, and flipped on the scanner. At half past, a female voice came across the airwaves:

"Units be advised. All I have is two gunmen running down Delmar Boulevard."

I quickly switched the station, picking up a male voice a fraction down the dial:

"I have a confirmed shooting at the 1600 block of Shepard Drive."

I called Alicia.

"Are you ready?" I asked.

She sounded tired.

"We have a crime scene. I'll meet you there."

"You what?"

"A crime scene," I said. "You wanted to go. We've got a good one."

"Really?" She seemed to come to life. "Where is it?"

On my way out to the car, I realized that she was a half-hour drive away and didn't know the city too well. But she'd find it; of that I was confident.

17

AT SIXTEENTH AND SHEPARD, everyone was gone. It had taken
me twenty-five minutes to get there, and now all was quiet, just a
strip of yellow police tape crossing off the entrance to a corner
store.

I parked in front of Lucky 7 Liquors and waited for Alicia, feeling stupid that I hadn't brought the scanner so I could find another crime scene. I turned on the radio on the off chance that
something up to the minute might come over the all-news AM
station, then a car pulled up, a gold Crown Victoria that glowed
chariot-like on the dilapidated street.

The driver rolled his window down. I didn't recognize him at
first. He wore a tam-o'-shanter too small for his head and was
smoking a long cigar. Three scanners were cranked up loud.

"Are you out buffing?" he asked, taking off the hat and tossing it
on the passenger seat.

It was Dr. Osborn, one of the ghouls.

"You know, scanner buffing, looking for crime scenes, trying to
make a buck on the side."

"I'm with the *Independent*," I reminded him.

"I don't understand buffers," he said. "You're too busy working to appreciate the drama. You lose your feel for the human
condition."

I looked down the street, hoping to see Alicia's Delta 88, but there was no sign of her.

Dr. Osborn turned up one of the scanners: "Units be advised. I have a shooting at the 2300 block of Cole Street. Second call."

"How did I miss that?" Osborn began rolling up his window.

"Wait a minute," I yelled at him. "Can I come with you?"

He waved me over, and I wrote a quick note to Alicia with directions to Cole Street, nine blocks away, and left it on the Gremlin's windshield.

When we rolled up to the crime scene, a tight cluster of flashing red lights, some of the crowd walked toward Osborn's car.

"They think we're undercover," he explained. "It's the Crown Vic. It gets them every time." When we parked in an alley and headed for the *whop, whop* of an arriving ambulance, Marshall Holman emerged from the crowd, too quickly for me to hide. For a second I thought I might sneak by, but then he caught a glimpse of me just as we were passing and twisted back around, grabbing my arm.

"Hatch!" He seemed far more happy to see me than I ever would have guessed. "It's about time!"

He sounded as if he had been expecting me.

"Your girl is a trip." He laughed. "I better watch out or she'll take my job. What's her name again?"

I had no idea what he was talking about. "What?"

"Your girl, whatshername, the budding journalist?" He was amused by how confounded I looked.

"Alicia?" I asked.

"That's it! Alicia. Hold on to her!" He smiled and walked away.

Dr. Osborn was tugging at my sleeve, leading me into the heat of the crime scene. The ambulance had stopped. A teenage boy was lying on a stretcher surrounded by paramedics. He was still alive, moaning, having been shot in the chest. The photographer, the little man with wild matted hair, jumped in and began taking pictures.

"Look at Lucas," Osborn said. "Right in there! Every time!"

A police officer walked up to Lucas and gently took his arm, saying, "Okay, that's enough," and pulled him away from the tight circle that had formed.

Lucas seemed satisfied, shooting off a few more frames as he backed away, bumping into Dr. Osborn.

"Did you see? Did you see?" he asked. "I'm the only one. No other stills around."

Osborn introduced me to Lucas, who didn't remember me. "He's with the *Independent*. That'll save you a phone call."

I told Lucas thanks but no thanks, that I didn't make those kinds of decisions. I gave him the number of the night city editor, whose name he already knew, whom he no doubt harassed on a regular basis.

As the paramedics lifted the teenager into the ambulance, someone laughed from across the circle. The crowd filled the space where the stretcher had been, and that's when I spotted Alicia. She was talking to a policeman who was smiling at something she'd said.

"Gordie!" She caught my eye. "You were here all the time!"

The doors of the ambulance closed, the *whop, whop* beginning again. The crowd parted as the ambulance crawled forward. Alicia put her arm around my waist, leading me away from Dr. Osborn and the rest of the group, half a block up to a church, where we sat on the steps.

"You wanted me to be on my own, didn't you?" she asked. Her face was lit up like a child's, glowing from the heat of the crowd. She was thrilled, intoxicated by the whole experience, looking at me as if I owned the night and had given her a part of it.

"What happened?" I asked.

She told me she had arrived at the liquor store as everyone

was leaving and the yellow tape was going up. I had forgotten how fast she drove; she'd probably beaten me by a good ten minutes. Lucas had been there and another ghoul with a scanner and they had tipped her off to the shooting on Cole. She had left straightaway, arriving before the police did. By the time Holman showed up, she already had the whole story. She knew he was with the *Independent* by his ID, so she had taken him aside and briefed him, every detail confirmed when he checked with the officers.

Most amazing was how much the police had told her. They said the shooting was gang-related, that it was a payback all the way, that they knew the kid — he was a multiple felon. There were two likely suspects: a cousin of his girlfriend, from a rival gang, and another kid called Smoot. They told her the names of the gangs involved, said it started with a turf war on another side of town. They gave her more for a small police story than any reporter could have hoped for.

"You were watching me, weren't you?" she asked with a sly smile.

And I went along with it, because that's how it was with Alicia; that's what she wanted.

"You did great."

She was exhilarated. She couldn't stop talking. "Did you see all the blood? It was unbelievable, like his heart had blown up."

She described the teenager in detail, the sounds he was making, the gurgle in his chest, the way his eyes rolled back, the sparkle of his diamond earring, his white shirt painted red, the blood, until finally I interrupted, "I was there. I saw it. I know what you mean."

"My daddy owned guns," Alicia said, as if an afterthought, and for a moment I remembered Texas.

The Delta 88 was parked nearby, and when she turned to me, her eyes wide and grateful, I had the sense that I held the power, that despite her newfound success, I was in charge.

"I think that's enough for one night," I said. "Let's get a beer."

I was caught in a role, waiting to see how this drama would play itself out.

Blueberry Hill was a crowded bar in the middle of the U City loop, with photos and memorabilia from the seminal artists of rock and roll. They had Chuck Berry's guitar and Muddy Waters's harmonica, LPs signed by Fats Domino, every wall covered with the conks and pompadours of 1950s idols. Alicia found a booth near the window while I got a pitcher of Budweiser.

"Crime reporting isn't so hard," she was saying. "I'm catching on fast."

I drank the beer quickly.

"Where do you think they'll put the story?" she asked.

I told her Metro, page 3, if anywhere. "Someone gets shot every day. You only make the paper if you die."

We talked about what makes a story a story, how the better part of the daily is already reserved, for politics and business, for local interests, for national and foreign news dragged off the wires, for sections like Obituaries that follow the ebb and flow, how there's only so much space each day for fires and car wrecks and homicides, things that come up unexpectedly.

"Gang shootings happen all the time," I explained. "Like anything, it's how rare something is that makes it a story."

I ordered another pitcher. Alicia had stopped drinking.

I talked about the country's increasing obsession with grisly news, its appetite for shock and psychopathology, and gave her an example from that morning where a housewife in Arizona went crazy, thinking her children were possessed by the devil. She shot them one by one as they got off the school bus.

"That story made national news. Front page, because she was a woman."

"Why?" Alicia asked.

"Because women don't kill," I said. "When a woman kills, it's big news every time."

When the late news came on, we moved up to the bar to watch Channel 8. Alicia was fixated on the television. I drank another beer. The news anchors looked blurry.

After sports and the weather, they cut to the shooting on Cole Street. Alicia grabbed my shoulder. "There I am, that's me." The teenager was being lifted into the ambulance.

"Did you see me?" she asked, as Channel 8 cut to a fire in East St. Louis.

"You were great," I said.

On the Inner Belt Expressway, Alicia was driving far too fast on mostly empty road. She was switching lanes, something she liked to do even when she wasn't passing cars. I felt dizzy, out of focus. The "New Car in a Can" that she had recently sprayed in the interior was making my stomach turn. I was sitting in the middle of the front seat, with the armrest up, not sure how I had gotten there. I looked at the empty passenger seat, thought of rolling down the window, but instead leaned closer to Alicia. The radio was on. A country-and-western station.

"Where are we?"

"Guess," she said, veering off the expressway. A green sign appeared on the side of the road: CITY OF ST. CHARLES.

"Home." And that's all I remember.

I woke up on the living room couch, startled by the cold emptiness of the room. The doorbell was ringing, amplified by the pounding in my head. The sun poured through the bay window. Alicia, in khakis and a white sweater, was standing at the front door.

"I'll call Clyde and tell him that you'll be over some time today," she was saying.

I couldn't see whom she was talking to, but the conversation had something to do with dogs. "He'll give you the updated records and everything. All you need is the pedigree folder, right?"

Alicia's back was turned and she was rummaging through a file box. I came up behind her and put my hands over her eyes. "Morning," I said.

She jumped. "Don't surprise me like that."

"Sorry." I stepped back. "What are you doing? Who's at the door?"

She was fingering the files, not looking up at me.

"That's the woman who's buying Gavin."

I hadn't seen the dog in almost a week. Alicia had sent him to Joe's farm the day before the painters arrived. I assumed he was still there.

"You sold him?"

"She paid five thousand dollars." Alicia sighed. "I don't have time for that kind of responsibility anymore, Gordie."

Alicia drove me downtown so I could pick up my car. I was already late for work. NPR was reporting from Bulgaria that Todor Zhivkov, the country's dictator for thirty-five years, had been replaced, his Stalinist government purged. She turned down the volume. "That's almost the end of it," she said. "Romania's next, then all the excitement in Eastern Europe should die down for a while.

"You know," she continued. "I have an idea for a story that'll make big news. I realized last night that I can become a reporter. It's all I ever wanted to be."

I was still groggy, thinking about the dog. I should have been pleased — Gavin was the last trace of Arthur — but the way that she'd just gotten rid of him made me uneasy. I thought of Joe scratching and nuzzling the dog and the Whitings' long history of champion wolfhounds, and I worried about how Margaret would take this last bit of news. She seemed already at a boiling point.

I was also beginning to wonder if there weren't some truth to

Margaret's theories about Alicia — her cold method of discarding the past, her transformations. I thought I loved her, but I knew from my experience with Thea that once distrust sets in, it has a way of becoming absolute.

At Sixteenth and Shepard, Alicia stopped the car to let me out.

"Then you'll help me with the story?" she asked.

"Of course," I said as she pulled away.

I walked toward the liquor store. The Gremlin was gone.

It took me until noon to get the car out of an impoundment lot and an hour more to clean up and take a taxi to the office. In my fog, I had forgotten to call Ritger. When I signed on to the computer, he had sent me a message: "You're a piece of work," it read. "Consider this a last warning."

Somehow I didn't take it seriously. I had given them fifteen months as a model employee. A few rough weeks couldn't do me in. I was going to Dallas and nothing could keep me.

18

MY FIRST DISAPPOINTMENT was flying into the international airport rather than Love Field. I hadn't realized that Dallas would
need more than one airport, so when the travel agent said Dallas–Fort Worth, I had assumed I would have the same descent as
President Kennedy had that clear November Friday, 1963.

Coming down the runway, I imagined my father packed behind
the fence at gate 28, surrounded by cheerful Texans and members
of the press. As the plane slowed, making its final turn, I thought
of the questions he was hoping to ask when the door to Air Force
One opened and the President descended the stairs.

I secretly hoped, even expected, to find myself at gate 28. There'd
be an enormous glass window with a view of the apron where
Kennedy's plane had sat, an exhibit nearby with the famous pictures — Jackie smiling in white gloves and her pink pillbox hat;
children holding signs saying ALL THE WAY WITH JFK; the young
handsome President, squint-eyed, waving to the crowd; the Lin-
coln Continental, top down, standing by to take him away.

I used to look for my father in these photographs: a corner of his
face, his profile, an arm and shoulder, the top of his head standing
among the press. It could have been he in a number of the pictures
that I'd seen in *Life* and *Look* magazine and in a book called *Four
Days to Remember*, which I'd kept on my desk at home.

I joined the midmorning traffic at gate 37 and stepped onto the moving walkway. That's when I noticed the sign for Dallas–Fort Worth International Airport. This wasn't Love Field. What's more, it was vast.

Instead of finding myself in the place I'd imagined, I was lost in a maze. I rode the walkway toward the rental car desk, ended up on the basement floor, and took the blue train, which left me at the Marriott Hotel. By the time I was finally out of the airport it was almost noon, and I had to be back for a six o'clock flight.

Sitting in my rental car near the corner of Elm and Houston, I looked across the street where the Book Depository used to be, now the Dallas County Administration Building. Horns blared, wide sedans hummed through the city. Even around noon, in the sweeping sprawl, Dallas was nothing but freeways and cars.

I had expected more. Because of what had happened here, I had thought it would remain a small city, intact, forever unchanged. A quiet memorial, a living reminder of what we had lost. That the city hadn't frozen in time, that it had grown bigger and newer and louder than anything I'd seen, unsettled me.

Weatherford, on the map, was clear across Fort Worth, an hour west. I would only have time to drive up Commerce Street, where my father's office used to be, before getting back on the highway to go see Jacqueline Steele. But when I spotted the sign for the museum, I couldn't resist stopping. It was spur of the moment, but I wanted to walk through and look at some of the pictures that landing at the wrong airport had denied me.

Many of the photographs I had never seen before, a whole series taken outside the Homicide and Robbery Bureau, office 317. My mother had often described this scene, the day after the shooting, when the ballistic tests were done and the case against Oswald was looking airtight. My father in his early articles had been one of the first reporters to voice doubt over the ballistic tests and the idea of miraculous marksmanship, suggesting the likelihood that more than one gunman must have been involved.

I scanned the crowd in the pictures: a corridor full of reporters and photographers gathered around Captain Will Fritz of the Dallas police. My father was a big man, six foot two and broad-shouldered, so he should have been easy to spot. But I couldn't find him amid the flashbulbs.

I approached the docent at the information desk, a woman around my mother's age with a friendly Texas accent.

"You must know the names of some of the journalists pictured over there," I began, then found myself hesitating. "Weren't there some famous ones who covered this case?"

"Yes, there were." She nodded. "Dan Rather and Jim Lehrer. A number of famous newspapermen got their starts here. What would you like to know?"

I stood there a moment, frozen.

"What would you like to know?" she repeated.

My mind was a blank. I wasn't sure exactly.

"We keep the archives in there." She pointed to a nearby room to be helpful.

I thanked her for her time and left the museum.

Jacqueline Steele's house in Weatherford was a brick rambler with Astroturf steps and a plastic birdbath on a recently cut lawn. The front door was open, so I called a hello through the screen. A woman appeared from the kitchen in a housedress and tennis shoes.

"Mrs. Steele? I called you on Monday. I'm the one who knows Alicia."

I could tell from the cross around her neck and her sweet droopy eyes that this part of the trip would not be in vain. She was a small woman with gray-blond hair, little curls on top. She had a sad face, the kind with a permanent frown, but something about her suggested she wouldn't close the door on me.

"I've come from Missouri," I said. "That's where Alicia is living now."

She was studying me through the screen: my pressed white shirt, my striped tie and khakis. I supposed I wasn't what she had expected.

"Has something happened?" There was concern in her voice.

"Oh, not to worry," I assured her as she led me into her dark-paneled living room. "She's a friend." That was my new tack, since the reporter approach hadn't worked before. I told her I knew Alicia because we were working on a story together, that I had been in Dallas on business and had some extra time.

"What's the story about?"

Without thinking, I told her it was about dogs. "We're both very fond of them."

"Dogs?" She frowned. "Alicia was terrified of dogs."

"Well, she loves them now," I said.

Mrs. Steele leaned back in her armchair. "I always liked them, but not Alicia."

We talked about nothing important, like the heat and her garden and how the actor Larry Hagman had grown up down the road. He was a local boy made good, she was saying, and he stayed close to home, a wonderful son to his mother. She brought me a glass of lemonade and offered me lunch, and though I was starving I told her that I'd already eaten. "Call me Jackie," she said after a while, and later, "Would you like to see Alicia's room?"

It was a two-bedroom house and Alicia's bedroom was in the back, still arranged for a twelve-year-old girl: dolls on the bed, pictures of horses on the wall, a pink vanity in the corner with a hairbrush and comb. I thought of my own bedroom, similarly preserved.

Sitting on the edge of the bed, Jackie flipped slowly through a photo album.

"She was a darling little girl, our only child," she said wistfully.

All the pictures of Alicia were from girlhood. She was towheaded, often in a ponytail, the kind of little girl whose socks were always clean. In many of the pictures, she was opening presents or holding a new toy.

"She was a darling. Everybody loved her until . . ." Her voice trailed off. Her broad brow, the way she held her head, reminded me of Alicia.

"What happened?"

She stood up abruptly, put the album in the closet, and pulled out another, handing it to me.

"This was hers. She left it here."

The first picture was of a boy, a skinny teenager, in a bright orange shirt from the 1970s, his long stringy hair the color of sand. His posture was slightly stooped, and he was standing next to a bunch of beakers in what looked to be a chemistry lab. The pages that followed were more of the same, the boy peering into his vials, sitting in a flimsy chair, pouring chemicals from jar to jar.

Alicia was in only one photo. She stood behind the table where the boy had been, resting her chin in her open hand, gazing into the camera. Her hair was long then, past her shoulders. She looked tired and sullen.

On the following page, the boy was lying on a slab of concrete, curled up like a caterpillar, death white, with red rims around his glazed-over eyes. The pictures, taken up close, were from all angles. There must have been twenty in all, the photo album ending halfway through with a front-on shot taken from the floor.

"What's wrong with him?" I asked, though I was pretty sure I knew.

Jackie Steele sat at the end of the bed, softly crying.

"We started to lose her when she met that boy," she said. "They thought they were Romeo and Juliet."

I had flipped through the pictures with amazing detachment, as if they were casket shots of Billy the Kid or mob figures from the thirties gunned down in the street, as if I were reading about some massacre on another continent, four hundred people with no connection to me, just lines in the newspaper, a grieving mother with her hands upraised. I had turned the pages with a macabre interest, not considering what the pictures might mean.

The story Jackie shared was about a bored, unhappy, gifted boy, the most promising student scientist in the region, who had somehow managed to catch Alicia's eye. He was her first love — she was only fifteen — and everything he said was gospel to her. He was three years older, a vast difference at that age, and he waited around for her, working at the Woolworth's instead of going to college.

Somewhere along the way, the two of them made a suicide pact.

"They felt they were too good for us," Jackie said. "They were too good for Weatherford and too good for the world."

The boy was a crackerjack chemist. He had won scholarships to attend a number of colleges, but on Valentine's Day, 1973, he poured two glasses of poison and drank the first one down.

"What happened to Alicia?"

Jackie was wiping her eyes with the collar of her dress.

"She thought better of it."

After the suicide, Alicia became a town pariah. The boy's parents thought her partially responsible, but no charges were ever pressed. She stayed another few months but dropped out of high school, and by the following June, she was gone.

For a while Jackie managed to keep track of her — she was working as a waitress in Albuquerque, selling Navajo jewelry in Taos; she had a government job in Denver for a time — but as the years went by and the letters were returned, it was clear that her daughter would never come home.

In the spring of 1987, when Howard Steele was dying of lung cancer, Jackie hired a private investigator to find Alicia. He located a phone number for an Alicia Whiting in St. Charles, Missouri, but when he called, the woman at the other end said her parents had been dead for years.

"He was the best private investigator in Texas," Jackie said. "He swore to me that it was her."

By the time I returned the rental car, I had only twenty minutes to catch my plane. By some stroke of luck the right train came first, dropping me off at terminal 4E just as the ticket takers were closing the door.

The plane took what seemed like a tour of the airport. I thought of the boy, those pictures, how they had almost looked familiar. But now the distance was closing fast. They hadn't come from a newspaper. I'd never seen them before. These photos were real, this part of Alicia's past undeniable.

Outside the window, the airport was under expansion, construction everywhere. Atop a long girder, a hundred feet in the air, stood a hardhat. As the jet engines roared, preparing for takeoff, the hardhat was walking toward the end of the beam. And he seemed to be suspended there, standing in the sky, oblivious.

19

WHEN I TURNED the key in my apartment door, it was unlocked. I panicked, rushing down to the building manager's office.

"I think someone's robbing me."

"You're kidding," he said.

He handed me the phone so I could call the police.

This part of St. Louis had become dangerous over the past couple of years. We'd had two thefts since I'd been here, one in the summer and one in October. Signs had been posted in the elevators and on the bulletin board about not opening doors for strangers.

"Did you see anyone?" he asked.

"No, but my door was unlocked. They're probably in there now, if they haven't already robbed the place."

"So you haven't been inside the apartment —"

I was dialing 911, telling him, "Those robbers are probably armed. I wasn't about to go in there."

The building manager was confused.

"And you're sure it's not your girlfriend? I let her in there around six o'clock. She said she'd lost her key."

"My girlfriend?" I hung up the phone.

"Yeah, your girlfriend. She's real nice."

"Right," I said. "Would you mind coming up with me, on the off chance that it's not my girlfriend?"

"Sure, I'll come up if you want. But I've been sitting here all day. Nobody got past me."

He followed me up to my apartment, standing behind me while I slowly opened the door and looked in.

"Hello?" I called out. "Anybody here?"

It was quiet inside. I turned the corner from the foyer, stepping cautiously into the living room.

The apartment was full of boxes. They were stacked two high, enough to cover half of the living room. Most were sealed, but a few had sheets and towels, kitchen appliances, knickknacks pouring out. In a daze, I went into the bedroom.

Alicia's clothes were strewn all over, on the bed, tossed over chairs, thrown in with mine in the open drawers of my bureau. I apologized to the building manager for the misunderstanding.

"I know how it is with women," he said. "Give them an inch and they take a mile."

Alone, I sat on the couch, small amidst the boxes. On the coffee table was a note, signed *A.A.W.:* "I took the scanner. Look for me on TV."

I was half asleep on the couch when Margaret called.

"I'm glad it's you," I said, and I meant it.

She told me that she was just calling, no reason, that she was having trouble sleeping at night, that her dreams had become increasingly terrible.

"Arthur's death is haunting me."

I'd been thinking about it too, I told her, even though I never knew him.

She asked me whether I'd made any progress with my research.

"I've just returned from Dallas," I said. "The strangest thing happened there."

I told her how I had gone to Alicia's mother's house, a humble little place outside of Weatherford, how her mother turned out to be a perfectly sweet woman. I said that we'd talked about nothing in particular at first until she began to trust me, showing me Alicia's bedroom and a couple of old photo albums.

"So, she handed me this second album," I said. "I opened it up and started turning pages, and then — you're not going to believe this, but there were pictures in there of a dead person."

I was speaking slowly, making no effort at drama, since drama was hardly necessary. "The dead person was Alicia's first boyfriend."

Margaret gasped.

"Several pictures of him, actually," I added.

I told her what Jackie Steele had said, how it was meant to be a double suicide, how the boyfriend was a bright young chemist who had mixed up some kind of poison, drinking it first with the understanding that Alicia would follow. "They were a couple of hopeless romantics. At least one of them, anyway."

"That's really quite something," Margaret said. "I'm returning to St. Louis tomorrow. We'll talk again soon." Then she hung up.

The intercom buzzed around half past ten.

"Who is it?" I asked.

"A friend," said the voice. It was a woman, but that was all I could tell. The voice was muffled, the sound of someone talking through her hand.

"A friend?" I was trying to sound coy. "Who's that?"

"A visitor," she said. "Come to pay tribute to a noble soul."

I pushed the button to buzz her in and paced the cramped living room, timing her ascent on the elevator to my apartment — doors opening on the first floor, past the second to the third, doors opening again.

I listened for her footsteps at the door, then stepped away, standing by the kitchen counter, where I could watch her come in and look less than surprised. My heart was beating fast. There was a knock at the door. Hadn't the building manager given her a key?

"Just a second." I walked to the door, deliberately slow, and looked through the peephole: outside were my mother and Thea.

"What are you two doing here?"

Part of me wanted to break down in front of them, tell them the truth from Alicia's first phone call, ask them to show me a way out. I was nervous now, not yet for myself, but in the way that a moviegoer gets nervous when the good guy's in trouble.

"What's going on here?" my mother asked, looking around. She picked an apron from one of the boxes and held it out in front of her.

"I wasn't expecting you until Friday," I said, stuffing what I could back into the boxes.

"Well, here we are!" She put down the apron, fixing her eyes on me. "We were hoping to surprise *you*, but it seems *you're* the one with all the surprises."

"Just a minute." I rushed into the bedroom and closed the door, throwing Alicia's clothes into the closet, stuffing her underwear and nightgowns and pantyhose back into my bureau drawers, kicking what was left under the bed.

My mother opened the bedroom door. "What's going on?"

"I thought you were coming in a couple of days," I said. "The place is a mess."

I was holding a pink satin bathrobe behind my back. I sat down on my bed, shoving the bathrobe under a pillow.

"We have this new reporter on staff," I began. "We just brought her in from Texas. She's on the investigative team, looking into . . . I think I told you already." I sensed that I was doing very poorly, that my face was turning red. "They asked me if I wouldn't mind storing her things for a few days while she found an apartment. She's a dynamite reporter. It was the least I could do."

My mother was looking around, then headed for the closet. I made an arc for the living room, cutting her off.

"You certainly do put up with a lot." She followed me out of the bedroom. "How do they expect you to live like this?"

I told her it wasn't so bad, that I'd been incredibly busy and hardly ever came home. "This reporter is a major talent and sometimes you have to make sacrifices for the good of the team." I tried to sound enthusiastic.

"And where is she staying, this reporter? Not *here*, I hope."

"Oh no, God no. They've put her up at a hotel. The Adams Mark — down by the river? She shouldn't be there long."

I was tapping on the kitchen counter, shifting back and forth. I was sure I could not have looked more guilty.

"And where were you planning on putting *me*?" my mother asked. "In that park across the street? Where? Out in the hallway?"

I shook my head. "I told you already — I wasn't expecting you until Friday."

Thea had been quiet the whole time, leaning against a wall.

"You can stay with me, Lorraine," she said softly. I could tell that Thea wasn't happy, that she was having trouble buying my explanation. "It looks like our timing was bad."

It was ten-fifty. I had to get them out of here.

"No, no," I said. "I'm extremely flattered . . . just surprised. I'm so happy you guys came early. It's just that my apartment's such a disaster."

"Well, it's a nice offer, Thea." My mother sat on the couch. "I don't see as I have much choice."

I was about to suggest that we all go out for a drink, that we figure out what to do next in a less cluttered setting, when Alicia burst through the door.

"You're back! What a night!"

She brushed past Thea into the living room and turned on the television, flipping to Channel 7, where a retired quarterback was pitching hassle-free loans.

"I'm on the news. And this time I got interviewed."

Alicia was flushed with excitement. She was wearing her khakis and white shirt and my baseball cap, with a gold *M* for the University of Missouri, turned backward.

My mother stood up from the couch, alarmed.

"Alicia!" I said, speaking loudly enough that I wouldn't be interrupted. "What a surprise to see you here! I didn't think you'd be back until *tomorrow*. You must have forgotten something."

She turned down the volume on the television.

"I was just telling my mother and my friend Thea that you're a new reporter with the *Independent* and you're working on a very important story."

Alicia turned around, noticing my mother and Thea for the first time, making no effort to acknowledge them.

"I said you've moved here from Texas and you're looking for an apartment in the city. It was the least I could do to provide storage for a few days while you found a suitable place to live."

Alicia brightened, seeming to recognize that she was in on a game.

"How's the Adams Mark?" I asked. "The hotel?"

"Oh, it's lovely," she said, not missing a beat. "I have quite a view."

She went into the specifics of her residence at the Adams Mark — decor, quality of service, convenience to downtown — showing remarkable skill at improvisation.

I introduced her as Alicia Whiting. Thea looked away.

"I prefer to be called A. A.," Alicia corrected me. "It's going to be my byline."

I was trying to figure how to get her out of the apartment and my mother and Thea to Thea's place without further trouble, but then the late news came on. The crime scene Alicia had come from was the lead story on the news, and she promptly forgot the game we were playing when the Channel 7 anchor cut to a multiple homicide.

"There I am!" She pointed at the television, giddy with excitement. "Look at me!" She was next to the screen, following her image as the camera panned around.

I tried to distract my mother and Thea with small talk, but they were watching Alicia.

"Listen!" She turned up the volume.

A reporter was questioning her at the scene.

"No, I didn't see it," she was saying, "but I was the first one here. These two were shot in the head. It was incredible. The backs of their heads were blown straight off."

My mother and Thea looked on in disbelief.

When Channel 7 moved to the next story, Alicia brought out some pictures.

"Lucas gave me these," she said. "It's that boy we saw the other day, the one with the hole in his chest."

She spread them out on the living room table.

"This one was done with a .38 Magnum. Look at that wound!"

She said she'd learned a lot about handguns in the past few days. She couldn't believe how fast and efficient, how powerful they were.

"My daddy kept guns. But I never knew what they could do."

"I don't like that woman," my mother said when I had finally managed to coax her and Thea out of the apartment and into the car. "Something's funny about her. I wouldn't trust her for a second. She's liable to keep explosives."

I was driving across town toward St. Louis University.

"She's a crime reporter," I tried to explain. "That's what they're like. They seem to enjoy it, but it's just a defense. It's the only way they can deal with the horrible things they see."

My mother was adamant. "I don't care what you say, Gordie. That woman's loopy. If I were you I'd have all the boxes removed and I'd sleep somewhere else. I can't believe you gave her a key."

I said it wasn't my idea. She got locked out while I was in Dallas and the building manager gave her an extra without my approval. "Dallas, by the way, was wonderful."

"We're not talking about Dallas!" My mother was leaning over my shoulder into the front seat. "We're talking about this crazy woman you just left alone in your apartment. Why didn't you kick her out when we left?"

I told my mother that I didn't need a lecture — I would have thought by now that she'd know enough about journalism to understand why Alicia was the way she was. Thea said nothing during the drive, and when I dropped them off, she wouldn't look at me.

"Happy birthday," my mother said quietly. It was a little after midnight. I had been born just before midnight of this day, twenty-three hours and some minutes from now, twenty-three years ago. I got out of the car and gave my mother a hug. Thea was already walking toward the building.

"I'm sorry," I said. "I'll see you tomorrow."

On the drive back to Soulard, dread set in. It dawned on me that my mother and Thea were good, that they had wanted to see me on my birthday, that this surprise they had planned was the most thoughtful and decent gesture. The closer I got to my apartment, the more alone I began to feel.

I took the elevator up to my apartment, and as the doors opened on the third floor, I watched myself appear, as I often did, in the full-length hallway mirror opposite the elevator doors — like an actor taking the stage.

Alicia was standing in the foyer of my apartment, a newspaper under her arm.

I braced myself.

"Happy birthday." She kissed me. "Did you look at the clock? It's after midnight."

I checked my watch, just for show. I was wondering what had gotten into her. Was this some kind of ploy?

"Did you think I'd forgotten?" She took both of my hands

and held them out in front of her. "What's wrong? Are you mad at me?"

I let go and walked into the kitchen and began putting things away. "No, I'm not mad." I hesitated. "Everything's fine."

"You must be upset about something. You're not acting like yourself." Alicia put the newspaper down on the coffee table.

"I know why you're mad. I embarrassed you, didn't I? Your mother must think I'm a crazy person, bursting in here with all that talk of blood and gore. I guess I didn't make the best impression."

Before I had begun reading Alicia's journals, I'd often imagined how nice it would be to introduce her to my mother. I had even brought it up with her. But now this idea of making a good impression was ridiculous.

Alicia came over to me and rubbed my back. "You didn't tell me that your mother was coming."

"I didn't know she was coming." It was only partly true.

"Well, I hope you're not mad at me. I admit I've been distracted lately, running all around chasing down stories." She went into the bedroom and looked for her clothes that I had thrown in the closet.

I followed her, slid open the closet door.

"I'm not mad." I put a handful of her clothes in my chest of drawers. Alicia slipped on a pair of my comfortable pants.

"Tomorrow's going to be a busy day," she said. "I'm going to bed."

I turned out the light in the bedroom for her and finished cleaning up the kitchen and living room. Seeing her boxes scattered across the floor of my apartment, I imagined the new owners of the house on Dalecarlia Drive moving in their furniture. Alicia had not so much as mentioned the boxes.

After tossing and turning on the couch, I went back into the bedroom. Alicia was asleep. She rolled lazily away from me as I slipped under the covers. I tried closing my eyes, but my eyelids fluttered, letting in the moonlight.

For a while I followed the shadows of cars across the wall. I had work tomorrow. My job was on the line. I thought of Thea and the mistakes I had made. I would have given anything to tell her I was wrong.

20

WHILE ALICIA was still in bed, I slipped out of the apartment the next morning, wearing the same clothes from the day before, and walked to work in the crisp fall air. It was my twenty-third birthday, and I had hardly slept.

The newsroom was empty. Jessie Tennant had signed off her computer. I looked over the faxes, glanced at the obituary page, then checked my mailbox.

Alicia had already called. "For Gordie Hatch, a.k.a. The Shadow," the switchboard operator had transcribed. "Imagine my surprise this morning to find that you had disappeared. How about calling me at the apartment and explaining yourself?"

A little later, Margaret called.

"That was quite a surprise," she said. "Why is Alicia answering your phone?"

I lowered my head into my hands.

"Remember how we talked about how she was ready to move? All those packed boxes?" I said. "Well those boxes have a new address. It's 2600 Missouri Avenue, Number 323 . . . She moved into my apartment."

"She did, did she? I can't say *that* surprises me. In fact, it sounds familiar."

"Well, when I returned from Dallas last night, she had literally taken the place over."

"Do something for me, Gordon," Margaret said now. "Be careful."

Alicia wasn't home when I called back, or at least she wasn't answering my telephone. So I went about my daily chores. The two o'clock meeting was over and still I hadn't seen Ritger.

My mother called in the middle of deadline, saying she had picked a restaurant near me in Soulard for my birthday dinner. I suggested it might be better if we went somewhere closer to Thea's.

"Thea won't be joining us. She'll be with her father. He's had a setback."

I was pulling together an obituary and didn't have time to go into it. "I'm sorry to hear that. I'll call you when I'm finished with work."

When I had checked the page downstairs, I kicked back and watched the conference room. The door was wide open. The fan was taking a break. The newsroom had a post-deadline calm to it, so I could hear what was being said inside. A group of editors were talking about the paper's upcoming endorsement for a vacant school board chair. It wasn't so much what was being said as the clamor over the decision that got my attention. It seemed that no two editors could agree until finally St. John stood up and took charge, marching around the table, bullying his choice through.

I had noticed before that the most powerful editors were the ones who spoke the loudest: St. John had risen on the volume of his voice, just as Ritger had fallen, silenced by his jaw. The hierarchy of the newsroom, it seemed to me now, perhaps the hierarchy of anything, had all to do with how loud one could raise one's voice.

When the meeting was over, St. John headed straight for my desk. "Meet me in my office." He sounded ticked off.

Ritger was leaning against the floor-to-ceiling window that overlooked the city. For a brief moment, I imagined him crashing through it.

"Sit down, Hatch," St. John said. "I think you know why you're here." He closed the door, then sat down behind his massive desk.

He went over my offenses one by one: the hours I'd wasted doing advancer pieces "on the company clock," how I'd cut out of work early "too many times to mention," the correction they'd had to run the week before, the "general carelessness" with which I approached my job. He spoke of long-distance calls to "cities all over the country" and other calls that had nothing to do with obituaries. He told me I was insubordinate, that I didn't believe in paying my dues.

"After that business with Bette Davis, I put Dick on the watch," he said. "I don't know what scheme you've got going, but there's no place for it here.

"We know about your sick day," St. John continued. "I hear the weather is nice in Dallas."

I knew where this was heading, but just as I recognized that I was about to hit bottom, I believed, for the first time, that perhaps I had a story. By instinct or accident I had been following a story all along, and now the *Independent* seemed unimportant.

"You've had a number of warnings, but you've chosen to ignore them," St. John concluded. "By the end of the weekend, I need your desk cleared out and your ID card."

He handed me a termination letter.

When I left the building at a quarter past seven, Alicia was waiting at the curb in the Delta 88. I was delirious from the spin of events.

"It's you." I looked in the passenger window.

"I have a front-page story." She had a manic look in her eyes. "Notify everyone. We're going to the conference room."

She got out of the car.

"Wait a minute," I said. "This is a bad time." St. John was still liable to be there.

"I have my story. I've thought it all through."

"It's really not a good time." I was exasperated.

"But I want to do it now," Alicia insisted, the whine of a child in her voice. "I've already done all the other stuff. You and I are going to write this story, Gordie, and it's front-page news. I know what it takes to make big news, and now I've got it."

I was shaking my head, partly to say no, mostly in disbelief.

"This is the moment. This is it. We have to seize the moment," she said. "I promised you I was going to do a big story, didn't I?"

I told her that we just couldn't do it yet; I had some important business to take care of. "Why don't you go out and find another crime scene," I suggested in desperation.

She looked frustrated, angry. "I'm tired of the scanner. I've chased down too many of those kinds of stories. You might be happy on page seven, but I'm not." She began to make her way to the building.

"Wait. Stop." I grabbed her shoulder. "I'll meet you here at eleven o'clock tonight, okay? We can do the story then," I said. "I have dinner with the executive editor and can't miss it. I promise you we'll make the front page."

She stopped and turned around, her restless look settling to a gaze. "Fine, then. I'll meet you at eleven."

I arrived early at the restaurant where I was meeting my mother for dinner. I waited by the window, read over the menu, made distracted small talk with the maitre d', then went to the men's room to clean up. At the sink, I washed my face and neck, slicked down my hair with water, tried unsuccessfully to press the wrinkles out of my clothing. Up close to the mirror, I checked my reflection for signs of trouble.

My mother was all dressed up in a new black dress and an embroidered shawl. She wore a string of heavy pearls with earrings to match and had on deep red lipstick. I had never seen her in such bright lipstick before.

The Roma was a midrange Italian restaurant whose moment had long passed, but it remained one of my mother's favorite places. She had come here with my father in the springtime during college. They'd taken off their shoes and stomped grapes in the garden, sung along with the piano player who had played the standards. But now the garden was closed for the season, the piano tucked away in a darkened room. The place was mostly empty. Our table was in the middle of the restaurant, though I had been hoping for a booth, where I could spread myself out, try to relax for later tonight.

"You don't look well, Gordie," she was saying. "I don't know what they're doing to you, but it's got to stop. You're wearing the same shirt you had on yesterday. You can't even pull yourself together in the morning."

I picked at my carbonara, which was rich and salty. I was eating too much bread, drinking more white wine than I had wanted to.

"It's not the same as it used to be," my mother said. "I'll give you that. There are too many Ivy League types in newspapers these days, too much cuteness. The real journalists, the ones who go out and get the story — they're few and far between."

She went on this way for most of dinner, which was a relief. It allowed me to drop out of the conversation. Lately time had accelerated for me, headlong into uncertainty, accelerated for Alicia as well. We were on the same clock, moving at the same speed, going, it seemed, in the same direction. She seemed truly to believe that she was a reporter on the verge of a breakthrough story. She had taken hold of my delusion and made it her own. When the road ended for me in St. John's office, and I realized that in a sense I had been pursuing a story all along, Alicia was right there with me, waiting at the curb to merge, two into one.

After the main course, the waiter brought out a plate of tiramisu with a single lit candle, and the few people left in the restaurant sang "Happy Birthday" to me. My mother leaned over and gave me a kiss, handing me a card with my full name, Gordon Charles Hatch, written on the envelope.

On the front of the card was a close-up black-and-white shot of a pair of old cowboy boots leaning against a post. Inside she had written, "A little something for your pilgrimage . . ."

The check was for three hundred dollars.

Later, when I dropped off my mother at Thea's, telling her that Alicia — A.A. — had found an apartment and was planning to move her boxes out over the weekend, she told me that she understood. I hugged her and thanked her for the evening. She said she was proud of me and insisted that I hurry home and try to get some sleep.

Driving off, I felt like a bastard for the three-hundred-dollar check in my pocket.

21

ALICIA WAS WAITING in the lobby in her khakis and white T-shirt and a pair of round tortoise-shell glasses that I hadn't seen before. She was carrying my father's briefcase. I thought about telling her that certain things were off limits but instead signed her in at the security desk, saying, "I didn't know you wore glasses."

"I don't." She took the glasses off, then put them on again. "I saw a reporter on TV who was wearing glasses, so I went to Osco's and bought these."

"Well, they look good." I was suddenly nervous.

"And I found this junky old briefcase in the apartment. I knew you wouldn't mind."

The doors of the elevator closed, then opened again, the gentle "Going up" cut off midsentence. An arm reached in and Jessie Tennant stepped inside, not noticing me at first as she pressed the button for the sixth floor.

Before I could say hello, Alicia said, "I'm doing a big story tonight. I've been telling Gordie that I'm sick and tired of writing all these crime stories. Everyone knows I'm better than that."

Jessie Tennant raised her eyebrows.

"My story is going to be front page," Alicia said, looking severe.

When the doors opened on the sixth floor, I tried to signal Jessie

Tennant to let her know that she shouldn't worry, I'd explain it all later, but I failed to get her attention.

Alicia headed straight for the conference room, walking fast, not looking around.

"We're doing the story here." She opened the door, waiting for me.

"How do you mean?" I asked.

"I mean we've got to do the story now and we're doing it here. We don't have all night."

"You can't write the whole story in the conference room," I said. "When I write a story, I do it on the computer, and there are no computers in here."

"Well, I don't know computers. And I want to do it right here, right at that table." Alicia sat down at the head of the glass table, St. John's place. "Why don't you get a tape recorder, then," she said. "Let's not get anything wrong."

"I guess I'll put the story on the computer later." I went to Marshall Holman's desk to find an extra tape recorder, wondering how I was going to finesse this.

The newsroom had mostly emptied out. A couple of copy editors were still at their desks, as well as the night city editor, who was dispatching Holman from crime scene to crime scene. The late crew, many of them demoted from dayside, were haggard looking, embittered, not a likely group to guard the sanctity of the conference room.

I found a tape recorder in the middle drawer and tested it, taking some extra batteries and tapes. On the way back I passed Jessie Tennant's desk, and whispered, "I promise I can explain this later."

Alicia was ready.

She had lined up several pencils and a notepad alongside an assortment of newspaper clips, different from the ones she had brought to Union Station. I noticed that my own envelope, the one with my advancers and Arthur's grid and notes from Jessie Tennant and Margaret, still sat undisturbed in the inside pocket of the opened briefcase.

I glanced over the clips. Alicia had clearly lost interest in features. This new batch held the kind of stories that lead off the evening news: shootouts, sieges, domestic tragedies.

I set the tape recorder on the conference room table, prepared to play along. "Ready?" I asked.

"Of course."

She adjusted her drugstore spectacles and pressed Record.

"This is A. A. Whiting." She leaned over the tape recorder. "The following account is my front-page story."

"Let's begin at the beginning," I said.

I had thought out how I was going to do this, rehearsed it at the Roma as my mother dispensed advice, though I realized my control was now limited. "I've done a little research," I began. "And I understand that in Weatherford, Texas, 1973, you knew a boy who was poisoned —"

She didn't seem at all surprised that I knew this. Instead, she corrected me. "Let's not say that I knew a boy who was poisoned. Remember, I'm the reporter and I've got to protect my source. It's one of the first rules of journalism."

"How do you propose to do that?" I asked.

"Let's just say instead, 'There was a girl who knew a boy who was poisoned.' We'll call her 'the girl' and we'll call him 'Phillip.'" A glassy look came over Alicia's eyes. The presence of the tape recorder seemed to be having a soothing effect on her. "Phillip was a scientist, and he performed scientific experiments in his lab in his basement."

"What kind of experiments?"

"I know what I'm doing, Gordie," she said. "First I wanted readers to know that his parents were divorced and he lived with his father, who was hardly ever home."

He used to mix poisons, she said, and test them out on small animals, mice and squirrels, cats, and eventually dogs from the next town over. "Four milligrams of ricin could kill a cat. Six milligrams could kill a dog, and anything after that could probably kill a person, but he didn't use ricin on people."

Phillip was working on a number of different poisons — some that killed slowly, the victim showing symptoms of a short natural death; others that took effect immediately, causing cardiac arrest.

"And how did the girl feel about Phillip killing animals? Didn't it seem barbaric?" I asked.

"She was just a girl. She hadn't been out in the world, so nothing seemed real," Alicia said. "And he was very convincing, very sure about himself. He put a lot of importance on the process of dying. He wasn't religious, but he did talk about the afterlife, how you had to be prepared." She was leaning over the table, speaking dreamily. "He thought if death catches you by surprise, then you have to relinquish a kind of eternal control."

The girl fell in love with Phillip. They were two people in a world that didn't understand them. He was a genius and she his assistant. The beginning of the end occurred when he took her to the film version of *Romeo and Juliet*, the one by Zeffirelli, shown downtown at the Mayfair Theater.

"He was Romeo and the girl was Juliet. The story was the most perfect romance ever told and they took it as a call to action, a personal message meant just for them," Alicia said. "They believed it was their fate to die together."

Outside pressures only strengthened Phillip's resolve — from his mother who lived in Dallas and had married a wealthy man, from his father who drank too much and wanted him out of the house, from people in town who saw him at the counter of Woolworth's and told him he was squandering his future. What he had not foreseen was that the girl might change her mind.

"She told him she would do it. She imagined herself doing it. She thought about drinking the poison and dying in his arms. But then the girl realized it was a bad idea." Alicia shook her head. "Besides, Phillip wanted to die. He was obsessed with death. Perhaps he didn't want to lose himself to the vastness of his own talent. Dying was a form of control."

By Valentine's Day, the girl had lost courage. "They went to the cemetery at dawn, to the mausoleum of a man named Robicheaux. Phillip said he thought Robicheaux was a romantic name," Alicia said. "They had the poison with them, in the pockets of their lab coats — four jequirity beans ground up in sugar water. Phillip drank his glass and the girl drank hers, but she had secretly switched her beans for hard candies."

"What did the beans look like?" I asked.

"They're half black and half red and about this big." She showed a space of less than a quarter of an inch between her thumb and forefinger. "They're the size and hardness of lentils, but rounder," she said. "They have this yellow stuff inside called abrin. It kills you."

She slid the notepad and pencils toward me. "Don't you want to write some of this down?"

"I can get it from the tape. How long did it take for him to die?"

"A couple of hours," she said. "Phillip loved jequirity beans because they're rare and pretty. In Mexico, they put them on rosaries."

I checked the tape. It was less than a third of the way through.

"For a long time the girl felt guilty about what happened," Alicia said. "For years after she left Texas she actually wished that she had followed through with the plan. But unlike Phillip, she wasn't so fascinated with death and had never considered suicide before meeting him. The fact is, if the girl hadn't come along, he was going to kill himself anyway. She is still convinced of that. The way she looks at it now, at least he was in love and thought he wasn't dying alone."

Alicia had little to add about the aftermath. She said that the girl lay with her eyes closed on the cold ground trying to distract herself by thinking of cartoons. Then she ran home and got a camera to take some pictures of Phillip lying outside the mausoleum, pictures she later put in a photo album which she had since lost.

"She thought it was important to capture that moment. She did it for him," Alicia said.

The girl would have left Weatherford right away, but she'd never been anywhere and didn't know where to go. The way she eventually did leave, and later left the other places she moved to, was by bus, going to the station and getting on the first bus out, regardless of where it was going.

I couldn't help but think of my father's trip to Dallas then, an eerie parallel.

"She got off at Albuquerque. It was the last stop," Alicia said.

I turned off the tape and excused myself, saying that I'd be back in a second, I had to use the men's room. Alicia nodded patiently, saying she'd wait.

In the men's room, I felt queasy. I leaned over the sink, thinking I might be sick. At the mirror, I touched my face, as if to make sure I was really there. My eyes were mapped with blood veins.

Outside the door, Jessie Tennant was taking a drink at the water fountain.

"That woman I've been talking to has a big local story," I said to her. "Don't mind what she said in the elevator. She's not all there."

Jessie Tennant nodded her head conspiratorially.

Alicia was sitting up straight, her superfluous glasses at the end of her nose, her blond hair in a high ponytail, a number 2 pencil behind her ear. For a moment, seeing her there, I felt sad. She was like a child, with her clear eyes, her serious, almost sweet expression, the way her small hands were folded on the table. I wondered if she just didn't know what she had done.

"Sorry to keep you waiting." I sat back down.

Picking up the tape recorder, my hands were shaking. I couldn't feel my fingers pressing Record. "And Arthur?" I asked, trying to make my voice sound strong.

Alicia was eyeing me pensively, pulling at her lip.

"Let's say that the girl became a woman and married an older man. She had kept her four jequirity beans, the ones she had promised to drink with Phillip. She had carried them from place to place, hidden among her things."

"Why?"

"I don't know. She just wanted to keep them," Alicia said. She took off her glasses and looked toward the ceiling, as if she were trying to think of something.

"But then her marriage goes flat. She realizes her husband loves someone else, that she will never be the primary woman in his life," Alicia continued. "She becomes angry. She tries to force her husband to love her, but he disappears into his work. The tension becomes so great that the husband threatens to leave. Now, let's say that the girl, the woman, loses her mind one day and grinds up the jequirity beans that she's been keeping. She puts them in his Gatorade. He always drinks Gatorade when he rides his exercise bike, and just like Phillip the husband dies."

She looked me in the eye. "Well?" she asked.

I said nothing.

"That would be a front-page story, wouldn't it?"

I couldn't stand the feeling of her eyes on me. "Yes," I said.

"Then you should type it in and move it to Print."

As we were getting ready to leave, Marshall Holman appeared at the conference room door. Behind him, the night editor was putting on his coat, making his way to the elevators.

"So you're here to take my job?" Holman said to Alicia.

She did not seem pleased to see him. "Why would I want your job?" she asked. "I have a story for the front page."

"Really?" Holman pulled up a chair.

It was a chance to excuse myself. "I'll be right back." I got up from the table and shut the conference room door, went to my desk, and looked up the home number of Margaret Whiting.

I felt compelled to call her. The news was too much to carry alone.

She picked up on the first ring.

"Margaret," I said.

"Yes." She seemed wide awake, though I knew it was getting late and she had work the next day.

"It's Gordon Hatch," I said quietly into the receiver. "I only have a second but I have to tell you something," and in the suspended moment that followed, I felt that she probably already knew.

"How did you find out?" she asked.

"She told me," I said.

"She told you?"

"She told me the whole story."

Margaret was quiet.

"I see," she said.

"My editors will have the story in the morning," I told her.

Out of the corner of my eye I saw the conference room door open and Holman attempting to leave. "I'll call you again," I said, adding — and I'm glad I did — "I'm so sorry."

I passed Holman on my way to the conference room.

"Your girlfriend's crazy. You know that, right?" he asked with a nasal laugh.

I ignored him and walked on, opening the conference room door. I turned off the tape recorder and told Alicia that it was a terrific story. I had no doubt it would go front page.

"You're a great reporter." I pocketed the cassette. "Congratulations."

"Will it be in tomorrow's paper?" she asked.

"Probably not tomorrow," I said. "There are a few things left to do with it. Maybe Saturday's, if that's okay?"

Alicia was packing her things into my father's briefcase, and she suddenly stopped. "It has to be in tomorrow's paper!" She was glaring at me. "You said it was going on the front page, and it's got to be tomorrow's!" She closed the briefcase and left the conference room, heading for the elevators.

"Okay," I said, catching up to her in the lobby. "Give me a second to drop off the tape with Rewrite. I've got to talk with the copy desk to be sure that everything is all set. I promise the story will be in tomorrow's paper."

I walked back toward the middle of the metro area and stopped behind a pillar so Alicia wouldn't see me.

I had no idea what to do.

I considered calling St. John at home. It was past midnight and he had fired me earlier in the day, but I had this tape sitting in my pocket, ready to back up the story. The last edition rolled off the presses at two-thirty A.M. There was still a bit of time, maybe, to write something quickly, a stand-alone brief on the front page promising further coverage in the next day's paper. I felt a wave of hope, followed soon after by more dread. It was absurd. St. John would hang up on me. Moreover, Alicia had not yet identified herself as the source.

I wondered if I could call the police and have them meet me at my apartment. I had all they'd need: the tape, the contents of my briefcase, her journals in the boxes crowding my living room. And I had Alicia herself, her craziness clear as day.

As I stepped into the elevator, still wondering what to do, Alicia linked my arm with hers. "We're going out dancing," she said. "We need to celebrate our front-page story."

She took me to a place called Quest, a crowded disco a little north of Laclede's Landing, with low ceilings and black lights that lit up our shirts and made our teeth look rotten. Glow-in-the-dark skulls covered the walls, bright-colored planets orbited the bar. Alicia pushed ahead, ordering me a whiskey and water.

"Let's have a toast," she said, standing on tiptoe to talk in my ear.

The place was loud, too loud for conversation, and it smelled of smoke and new plastic. We were standing at the edge of the dance floor, caught in the strobe light, getting pushed toward the middle. Alicia was dancing, moving with the music, flashing at me in stills with the pulse of the strobe.

The music had an industrial sound, the same metallic beat over and over, one endless song interrupted by howls and screams and sound bites of radio-era propaganda, a futuristic kind of music, self-consciously anonymous.

Alicia brought me a second drink, another whiskey and water. I was sweating and thirsty. I drank it fast, the bourbon rushing to my head.

We were dancing close. She had one arm around my waist; her eyes were closed. In the heat, the flashing light, in my delirium, I turned her around, ran my hands over her shoulders and arms. Face to face, she looked into my eyes, then away — thoughtful, bored, intense, remote — still frames flashing in the darkness.

Her back against a steel column, she pulled me toward her, tucked her fingers under my belt. A warbled voice screamed over the giant speakers, three words in another language repeated a hundred times.

Alicia let go of me, and in the next still I saw the back of her head, her profile opening up in slow motion, then the faces of a stranger, each more remote than the last, strobe light flashes of Alicia turning cold.

"We have to go home," she said in my ear, and turned away.

We drove in silence, south along the river back toward my apartment. It was past two o'clock. We had been dancing for a couple of hours.

She was slouched in the driver's seat, speeding along, flying through yellow lights and through a red light at Market Street. At Busch Stadium she turned west, swinging by the *Independent*, where she pulled up to the curb and parked the car.

"Can we get a paper?" she asked.

I hedged. "Why would you want to do that?"

"We have to read my article," she said cheerfully.

"The paper won't be up for another hour," I said, hoping she wouldn't notice the distributors lined up in the alley loading the final edition into their trucks.

Alicia threw the car into drive and peeled away.

"The story is great," I said. "Don't worry, you can see it in the morning."

I tried to imagine what was going on in her head, whether it occurred to her that her taped confession would have repercussions beyond the printing of the story. She must have realized that something was going to happen out of this, something beyond a "breakthrough" in her "career" as a journalist. And then I thought that, like "the girl" in her story, she must have no sense of consequences.

We passed under I-64, minutes from my apartment.

"After this, we won't be doing any more stories together," she declared, staring over the wheel. "I'm on my own now. I have ambition."

She shot through another red light. I slid my arm over, unlocked the passenger door, turned my body so I could see the whole of her.

She pulled over and stopped in front of my building.

"They'll tow you if you park here," I said, as if that might change the course of events.

"I park where I want to," she said.

I followed her to the entrance of my building, where she pulled open the front door.

"It's unlocked," I said stupidly, and followed her into the lobby.

My last reserves of energy were pouring through me. The elevator doors closed and Alicia pressed 3. How would I call the police with Alicia in the apartment?

We were separated by three feet. I was trying to look casual, leaning in the opposite corner.

I thought about grabbing her, wrestling her to the ground, calling for help. I wondered if I could stay up another night, another eight hours, without drifting off, defenseless.

The elevator stopped on 3 with a jolt. Alicia got out first. I let her go ahead of me, watching her in the full-length hallway mirror.

What I saw, then, was not Alicia, but her reflection.

The first shot sent her sprawling backward.

The second, an instant later, hit her in the chest.

I froze, my head suddenly empty as the elevator doors began to close.

Instinctively, I pushed L.

But as soon as the doors closed, they opened again, and standing in front of me, in a black dress and wire-rimmed glasses, holding her hands at her sides with the handgun pointed safely down, was Margaret Whiting.

22

THEA'S FATHER DIED two weeks later, and I went home to Columbia for his funeral. The funeral was on a Monday. St. John told me I could take as many days as I needed. At home, my mother had framed my clips, now hanging on the dining room wall — three front-page stories on Alicia and Arthur Whiting and two metro pieces as well as a brief mention in the *Washington Post*'s "Around the Nation" box.

These days it was so rare for a woman to poison her husband that the story had an old-fashioned, gothic appeal. One reader had written in a letter to the editor that it's a shame we live in a society where women have become as brutish as men, using guns and knives, even blunt instruments to dispose of their mates. "Thank you, Alicia Whiting," the reader had concluded.

I'd had some local fame. A couple of people had stopped me on the sidewalk, called me by my name. I'd felt eyes on me in the checkout line at the grocery store, had seen my face on television. Channel 7 had done a feature, and my refusal to be interviewed only added to the interest in my story — Obituary Writer Trapped in Black Widow's Web.

In the confusion of days that followed Alicia's death and Margaret's arrest for second-degree murder, through my return to work and a week and a half of stories with my name on the byline, when everyone in the conference room actually cared about my opinions, there hadn't been a moment to step back and make sense of what had happened.

When I walked in the door at 102 La Grange, the first thing I did was take down my stories. My mother would throw a fit, but it didn't matter. I couldn't stand to look at them. Lying in bed in the middle of the afternoon, an afternoon of Indian summer the day before Daniel Pierson's funeral, I was thinking of Alicia, as I had been every hour of every day since her shooting.

After the police had left, I had gone back through Alicia's belongings and found under my bed her envelopes containing newspaper clips, crime scene notes, and a journal that the police had somehow overlooked and that covered February through November, 1989. I took a good part of the afternoon mustering the courage to open the journal, knowing I would have to use it in the stories I was writing. I had already filed my third article in three days, and the journal confession would likely stand on its own as a final confirmation that "the girl" from the tape was, of course, Alicia.

But when I turned to the back, to Wednesday, October 2, expecting a long, detailed account of how she had ground up the poison beans and mixed them into her husband's Gatorade, I saw, in her child's scrawl, only these words: "Arthur died today. He was riding the exercise bike when his heart gave out on him."

Because there was nothing definitive about this or about the other journal entries she had written in the aftermath, I chose to ignore what their brevity, their omissions might have implied. I went ahead and filed my fourth story, detailing Alicia's past relationships and what I took to be my role in the narrative of her death: "Alicia had a particular gift," I wrote in the article, which ran on the front of the metro section. "Like a convex mirror, she was the augmented reflection of the man she was with. When I thought I was falling for her, I was falling all the more for my own journalistic dreams. Which is why this story does not belong to me. Finally, it belongs to Alicia."

My mother woke me for dinner.

"Why did you take the articles down?" she asked.

"I don't want to talk about it," I said.

"You're tired, I know." She patted me on the shoulder.

We ate our pasta without talking. I wasn't in the mood for conversation, and something was different about my mother. She was quiet, patient, deferential. I felt like the husband after a long day, sitting across the table from his agreeable wife. And it made me uncomfortable.

"When do you think you're going back?" she asked.

"I don't know."

The police had let me call Jackie Steele the night Alicia died. It had been my first thought when they brought me to the station for questioning.

She was groggy — it was three A.M. — and it took her a few seconds to make sense of who I was. I said I had terrible news.

"Alicia?" she asked.

"Yes," I said, and that was all she needed to know.

I told her I'd do anything; I could send home all the boxes, help her make funeral arrangements.

"I'd like to bring her home," she said.

Alicia was buried next to her father in the Weatherford Cemetery, under a three-by-five-foot headstone with "Alicia Steele, Our Darling Daughter" incised across it.

I visited Margaret at the St. Louis County Jail a week after the shooting. I had asked Joe to come along, but he'd told me no, he had already been to visit her; he would go only on Mondays.

"This isn't an interview," I said to Margaret. "I'm just here to see you."

"You shouldn't worry about me," she said. "I know a reporter from a friend."

Margaret looked washed out in her orange prison jumpsuit, but her spirits were high and I got the sense that a tremendous burden had been lifted. She had a self-possession about her, an aura of calm.

We talked about jail, her daily life, where she thought she'd be transferred to, the dates of the trial, if it was likely to go that way. I said I had full confidence in her attorney. He was one of the best in the city, and the evidence on the tape couldn't be more clear. I told her what the attorneys at the paper had told me, that the half-hour trip between St. Charles and my apartment was not enough time for premeditated murder. She'd get manslaughter in a plea bargain — four to six years — and if it went to trial she had a good chance for acquittal.

"You'd have enough public support," I said. "The D.A.'s office has nothing to gain."

I talked on and on, telling her what she already knew, details her attorney no doubt briefed her on several times a day. I guess I was afraid to stop talking, afraid that she'd see something awful in me. When at last I had run out of words, Margaret leaned forward and spoke into the grate.

"Alicia killed my brother," she said. "Whatever happens, I have no regrets."

Not a day after visiting Margaret, however, after the last of my major stories had run, I was in my apartment taking one last look through Alicia's boxes. I had promised to send her belongings to Jackie Steele in Weatherford, and I wanted to be sure that they contained nothing upsetting.

The police had seized the journals as evidence, all but the one I had later found under my bed, which I supposed I should turn over to the authorities as well. Before the police had arrived, I had already glanced through most of her journals, including the one from 1973, when Alicia and the boy chemist, whose name did turn out to be Phillip, were doing their experiments. Her entries corroborated her conference room confession almost to the word, which I had noted later in one of my articles.

When I had sealed and addressed all but one of the boxes, I considered Alicia's journal entry from the day Arthur died, the innocuousness of it, and decided to look at it one last time.

As I was flipping toward the last pages, an envelope fell out onto my apartment floor. It was a number 10 envelope, wrinkled and yellowed, unmarked except by the stains of age. I picked it up from the floor and turned it over. It was still sealed. I held it up to the light and could see, gathered at a bottom corner, what looked like tiny pearls.

I took a knife out of my kitchen drawer and cut open the envelope. Inside, all in a row, were four black and red beans. I poured them out onto the counter, where they plinked and rolled jollily around.

Daniel Pierson had died in his sleep.

I hadn't talked to Thea since the night Alicia moved into my apartment. When she called me at work with the news, I went to the men's room, locked myself in a stall, and cried.

Ritger was pleased when I handed him the twelve-inch obituary detailing Daniel Pierson's acts of valor in Vietnam. He made Thea's father the lead obit in the Sunday paper, with a photograph. It was the last obituary that I'd write.

After the burial, Thea came over to my house. My mother left us alone, saying she'd be back in a little while, and we sat in the dark living room, not bothering to open the blinds. Neither of us could find much to talk about. I got up and made tea because it was something to do.

Finally I said, "I've been incredibly selfish. I was so caught up in my own crises. I had no idea."

"I know, Gordie." She twirled the tea bag in her cup.

I had more to say.

"When you asked me what happened between us I didn't tell you, because I was mixed up and stupid and my imagination had gotten the better of me." I couldn't look her in the eye. "I thought you had found someone else. I was convinced of it."

"Why didn't you say something?" She looked up from her tea.

"I tried to," I said. "I was so sure I was right. I couldn't think to speak."

"You can't keep everything to yourself, Gordie. When you keep everything to yourself, eventually the secret will turn on you and make you crazy. He was a friend. You know that now."

I said nothing for a minute, then, "It turns out I do have a secret to tell you." I leaned back against the metal of the kitchen doorjamb.

"I found out something a couple of days ago that's turned my whole life into a joke." Thea and I had never talked about Alicia, but I knew from my mother that Thea had read all of the articles. "You know those four jequirity beans that she had been saving, the ones that she presumably used to poison her husband?"

Thea nodded.

"Well I was searching through her things and I found them," I said.

Thea set down her tea. "So she didn't do it," she said, almost a question.

"I don't know. She confessed to it. Now I don't know," I said. "The envelope that I found them in was old, too, like it hadn't been opened since 1973."

"She still might have done it, Gordie. You can't be sure. Maybe she had an extra stash of those beans."

"But I read her journal entry from the day her husband died, and she says nothing about killing him," I said.

"Okay, then why did she confess?"

"Maybe the story became more important than anything," I said, to myself as much as to Thea.

I hadn't planned to tell anyone about finding the jequirity beans, certainly not my mother or my editors. I'd already written five articles, and this latest discovery might force me to recant. But worse than that were the broader implications of Alicia's possible innocence. Margaret might have killed her, but I was the one who had set the events in motion.

"So what are you going to do?" Thea asked.

"What should I do?"

Thea walked over to me. "No secrets," she said.

Then she got her coat, touched my shoulder, and made her way to the front door.

I followed her out and sat down on the front steps, watching her.

She started the car, lowered the sun visor, and pulled out into the road. As she turned up the street ahead, I thought I saw her look back at me, and for a moment I felt something like hope.

Back in the house, I picked up Thea's teacup and held it against my cheek, where it still felt warm. Removing the funeral program from my pocket, I took off my tie and blazer and went wearily into my bedroom, laying my clothes across my writing desk. I noticed again the pictures on the wall, of my mother on her wedding day, of Harry Truman and his big gray smile, and the one from my uncle's yard taken when I was five years old. I leaned back against the bed and stared at the picture of myself in my father's shadow.

It came to me then what Thea had meant when she talked about the danger of secrets. I went into my mother's room, over to the rolltop desk that had been closed to me for eighteen years. I tested it and it pushed back easily. When had my mother stopped locking it?

There was a stack of mementos: my father with a flattop in a yearbook photo, his face rough from adolescence; a picture of him on an aircraft carrier saluting, holding a mop over his shoulder as if it were a rifle; a shoebox full of letters sent to my mother's address in Missouri and her parents' house in Indiana; an announcement of my birth — eight pounds, two ounces — a "future Hall-of-Famer."

Next to the overflowing shoebox was a monogrammed lighter, a ring of keys, a pair of reading glasses, and my father's wallet, thick with ticket stubs from White Sox games, grocery coupons, dozens of old receipts. In the billfold were two fives, a one-dollar bill, and a union card from the Newspaper Guild. His Illinois driver's license said he was five foot ten, 175 pounds.

And tucked in between all these things was a Ziploc bag safeguarding my father's obituary.

> Charles Hatch, a typesetter for the *Chicago Tribune,* died Sunday at Mercy Hospital of a malignant brain tumor. He was 36.
>
> Mr. Hatch was born in Wichita, Kansas, and briefly attended the University of Missouri–Columbia before joining the United States Navy in 1959. He was posted at New London, Connecticut, Norfolk, Virginia, and in the South Pacific.
>
> After leaving the Navy, he attended Hamilton Technical College in Indianapolis. He moved to Chicago in 1963, where he was hired by the *Tribune* as a typesetter.
>
> He was a member of the International Typographical Union and a contributing editor of the Chicago area ITU newsletter.
>
> Mr. Hatch leaves his wife, Lorraine, and a son, Gordon, of Chicago, as well as a brother, Thomas, of Wichita, Kansas.
>
> A funeral service will be held at 11 A.M. tomorrow at St. Bridgid's Church in Oak Park. Burial will be in Oak Park Cemetery.

The obituary ran in the *Chicago Tribune,* five and a half inches, no subhead.

I was sitting on my mother's bed reading it a second time when my mother came into the room. She stood in the doorway, in the crinkly black dress she had worn to Daniel Pierson's funeral.

"I'm so sorry, Gordie," she said softly.

I put my father's obituary back inside the bag and returned it to the desk with his wallet and lighter, his glasses and keys. I restacked the pictures in the order I had found them.

"It's okay, Mother," I said, leaving the desk open as I turned and left the room.

Later that evening, I made two grilled cheese sandwiches and heated up a large can of tomato soup.

"You've made dinner?" my mother asked, emerging from the back bedroom, where she had been all afternoon.

"I did." I placed soup spoons and napkins on the dining room table.

She sat down, unfolding her napkin.

"What would you like to drink?"

"Water's fine," she said.

"You've got a bottle of wine. Wouldn't you like a glass?" I opened it and poured two glasses of red wine.

"Wine, then, I guess." She smiled.

I brought the plates and bowls and glasses of wine to the table and sat down. I looked at my mother eating in silence, her black hair falling in front of her face.

She sniffed, wiped her eyes with the back of her hand.

"I want you to know something," I said. "There's no sense going into it now, but I do understand why you thought those stories were necessary."

She looked up, and I could tell that she wanted to respond but could not.

"Thank you for dinner," she said.

❖ 23 ❖

MY FINAL DAY of testimony at Margaret's hearing, as a witness for the defense, was blustery and cold. The day before, the temperature had reached sixty. Now snow was in the forecast. The *Independent*'s attorney told me to say nothing as we walked out of the courtroom and made our way down the hallway to the elevators. "Just ignore the questions and push on."

From the stairs I saw the small crowd of reporters and TV people waiting beyond the doors. Outside, the sky was pale purple, turning gray. The dying light brought things closer, into sharper focus: the French façade of City Hall across the street, the texture of someone's wool overcoat, my own face reflected in a wide-angle lens.

I sometimes used to picture this scene, flashbulbs and cameras, microphones dropping in, a closing circle, the strange feeling that came of being surrounded. The day after Christmas, I had seen myself on television descending these steps, and courtroom sketches of me with rosy cheeks and a lopsided face nothing like my own. On one station, these images followed photographs of Nicolai Ceausescu, eyes open, executed by firing squad.

A girl, I guessed in her late teens, was running up the sidewalk toward the courthouse. She wore a red turtleneck sweater and a white parka, and she was waving as she ran. Her skin was luminous, her cheeks full of color, a mist of perspiration over her face.

"Mr. Hatch," she called, out of breath, "I have a question."

Her pale eyebrows were raised, her blue eyes expectant. "Just one question, Mr. Hatch."

"No questions!" my attorney said.

But the girl could see an opportunity in my response, the way I stopped as she ran up to me, the look on my face as if I were trying to place her.

"I want to know about the stories you wrote in November — the first ones, from the week after Alicia Whiting died," she said. "Were they true?"

One of the reporters was stepping in front of her. The others called out questions of their own.

I turned to face her. "I believed them," I said.

She seemed satisfied. "I see," she said, and doing her best to sound like the other reporters crowded around me, like interviewers she had watched on television, she added, "That will be all, thank you." There was something sweet about it, the way she shrank, as if recognizing the false ring of her words.

The sky was darkening; the smell of snow was in the air. I crossed Market to Memorial Plaza, where the Gremlin was parked by a young tree.

"I'll call you," my lawyer said.

Up the road, a light had turned green and cars were pouring across Market Street, leaving what was left of the reporters stranded on the other side. I pulled out, driving west, away from the river.

I rubbed my hands together and switched on the heat. The old fan flapped and rumbled, coughing out warm air. A light snow had begun to fall, melting on the windshield, and the Gremlin filled with the smell of engine oil, as it had those winter mornings when I set out in darkness to deliver the news.